CAUGHT IN CUPID'S NET

Sarah Harper was very angry when a handsome young man in a flashy sports car stole the parking space in London that she was just about to reverse into. She gave him a good telling-off, but he just smiled and walked away. When Sarah's boss sends her to Sir Hugh Drayton's mansion in Cornwall to restore some valuable paintings, she is shocked to discover that the cheeky driver is Sir Hugh's son, Rhett. Is there really such a thing as love at first sight?

DEBORAH BLAKE

CAUGHT IN CUPID'S NET

Complete and Unabridged

LINFORD
Leicester

First published in Great Britain in 2001

First Linford Edition
published 2003

British Library CIP Data

Blake, Deborah
Caught in cupid's net.—Large print ed.—
Linford romance library
1. Love stories
2. Large type books
I. Title
823.9′2 [F]

ISBN 0–7089–4905–3

Published by
F. A. Thorpe (Publishing)
Anstey, Leicestershire

Set by Words & Graphics Ltd.
Anstey, Leicestershire
Printed and bound in Great Britain by
T. J. International Ltd., Padstow, Cornwall

This book is printed on acid-free paper

SPECIAL MESSAGE TO READERS

This book is published under the auspices of

THE ULVERSCROFT FOUNDATION

(registered charity No. 264873 UK)

Established in 1972 to provide funds for research, diagnosis and treatment of eye diseases. Examples of contributions made are: —

A Children's Assessment Unit at Moorfield's Hospital, London.

•

Twin operating theatres at the Western Ophthalmic Hospital, London.

•

A Chair of Ophthalmology at the Royal Australian College of Ophthalmologists.

•

The Ulverscroft Children's Eye Unit at the Great Ormond Street Hospital For Sick Children, London.

You can help further the work of the Foundation by making a donation or leaving a legacy. Every contribution, no matter how small, is received with gratitude. Please write for details to:

THE ULVERSCROFT FOUNDATION,
The Green, Bradgate Road, Anstey,
Leicester LE7 7FU, England.
Telephone: (0116) 236 4325

In Australia write to:
THE ULVERSCROFT FOUNDATION,
c/o The Royal Australian and New Zealand
College of Ophthalmologists,
94-98, Chalmers Street, Surry Hills,
N.S.W. 2010, Australia

1

'Oh, blast!' Sarah said aloud as she passed an empty parking space, a rarity in London these days.

Traffic hooted at her as she pulled over to the left and watched in her rear-view mirror for a gap in the traffic so that she could reverse back into the space. Ignoring more hoots from irate drivers, who were swerving around her dramatically and glaring angrily, she edged her car back towards the space. Two car lengths from the gap she watched in utter dismay as a red sports car nose-dived into the space without too much manoeuvring.

'Of all the cheek!' Sarah muttered under her breath. 'That has just got to be a male driver.'

It had been a long day and Sarah was tired. All she wanted was to get to her favourite bookshop, Samsons, before they closed. Normally she would have just shrugged her shoulders and driven off to find another place to park. She wasn't one to cause a scene, but, completely out of character, she stopped her car, got out, and stormed over to the other driver who was just locking his car door. He barely glanced at her as she approached him with her brown eyes flashing wildly, preparing for the inevitable confrontation.

He was dressed smartly but casually in black jeans, brogues and a black padded jacket. An onyx ring on his right hand glinted as he set his car alarm and pocketed his keys.

'What a perfect gentleman you are!' she said sarcastically and he looked up with a faint smile on his puzzled face.

'Thank you,' he said, 'but what have I done?'

'How could you fail to see that I was reversing down the road into this space?' she spat out. 'Just because you're male and you've got a flash car, I suppose you think you have priority over all the parking spaces. That was totally ignorant of you!'

'Excuse me!' he said indignantly. 'There was no one reversing into the space when I spotted it. How far down the road were you exactly? Huh? Women drivers! You should be a bit more observant. It's very bad practice to reverse half a mile down a busy main road with traffic racing towards you! Have you got a death wish or something?'

'Half a mile!' Sarah shouted, oblivious to the passersby who were watching the proceedings. 'I was not half a mile down the road, I was . . . '

He raised his hand to stop her in mid-sentence.

'I think perhaps you ought to move your car now,' he said patronisingly. 'It seems to be causing an obstruction, and there's a traffic warden walking this way.'

Sarah looked up to see the familiar uniform heading towards her car, and as she turned back to hurl a final insult to the man, she was even more furious to see him sauntering off. Seething, Sarah returned to her car and drove off, disappointing the traffic warden who was no doubt preparing to book Sarah for double parking.

'Men!' she hissed, and she drove down yet another side road, thinking, at this rate I'll be miles from the bookshop before I find a space, and probably out of petrol, too. She heaved a sigh of relief as a car pulled out of a space ahead of her.

'Cheers!' she said aloud.

A few minutes later, the bell tinkled above the door as Sarah entered the second-hand bookshop.

'Hello, Mr Samson,' she said to the short man sitting behind the counter.

His head was almost on a level with it as he looked at her over his spectacles and, smiling, muttered a reply as she made her way to the section marked History. She was a frequent visitor to the shop. Although it looked very small from the outside, it was a rabbit warren of shelves inside, containing hundreds of volumes. Sarah wandered up and down the narrow gangways flicking through the books, looking for some interesting titles to add to her collection. She didn't notice him at first, then, through the gaps in the shelves Sarah noticed a man emerge from another section with four books in his hands. The signet ring on his right hand flashed familiarly.

Mr Red Sports Car, Sarah thought, surprised by her sudden interest and concerned that her heart was racing rather unnaturally. She craned her neck and watched him pull a wad of notes from his wallet and pay for his books. In her anger with him earlier she hadn't noticed just how attractive he was. Now, hiding amongst the shelves, she stared at him from between the old volumes and couldn't take her eyes away from him.

He was tall and broad-shouldered, with thick dark hair curling sensuously round the nape of his neck. His tanned skin was taut against his strong jaw and chiselled cheekbones. Sarah was aware that her stomach had dropped into her shoes and regretted her undignified clash with him in the middle of the road earlier. Whatever must he have thought?

She watched him leave the shop and felt strangely deflated after he'd gone. The shop was suddenly cold and uninviting. All that remained was the faintest smell of his expensive after-shave mingled with the odour of musty books. The unlikely mixture made Sarah feel light-headed and a little faint.

She quickly paid for her book and left the shop, glad to be back out in the fresh air. She scanned left and right hoping for another glance of the stranger but it was as though he had vanished into thin air and this left Sarah with the very dismal prospect of never knowing him, and the surprise of how depressed this made her feel.

* * *

Sarah drove her car through the old, wrought-iron gates and entered a small courtyard. Parking in a space reserved for staff she dragged herself reluctantly out of the driver's seat. Work was far from her mind that morning and she had even contemplated phoning in with a headache, but decided against it. Martin would have been annoyed if she hadn't turned up today when they were so busy.

She glanced around the carpark and spotted Martin's black saloon in its usual place. He was in early, she thought, locking her car. She made her way across the courtyard and entered the old building by way of an impressive arched doorway nestling beneath a host of oriel windows. A polished plaque to the right of the door announced, HOLBERNS, established 1855.

The Holberns were a local family who had first opened up a museum in the middle of the nineteenth century, storing and displaying works of art and china and by the 1960s they had established themselves as one of the leading firms in the city specialising in renovation and restoration, as well as running very successful auction rooms. Sarah had completed a three-year course and had been working at Holberns for six years as a restorer and renovator.

She loved her job but of late was feeling disillusioned with life in London. It wasn't as glamorous as it appeared and she felt unsettled. She wasn't really going anywhere. That morning she had risen and had just not wanted to go into work and she didn't know the exact reason why except that she felt depressed. Perhaps she needed a holiday. The speed of life in London, it seemed, had caught up with her and she felt strangely apprehensive about the future.

She was twenty-eight and no nearer settling down with anyone than she had been ten years ago, and if the truth be told, the man she had bumped into the previous day had disturbed her. She had found herself thinking about him at home during the evening.

She soon busied herself rattling bottles of solvents and brushes, preparing for the day's work. She was working on an old oil-painting of a ballet dancer practising at the bar. There was some damage which she was repairing.

Her friend and colleague, Amanda, made her way over to where Sarah was working and peered at her with a furrowed brow, as though an intense inspection would somehow reveal what was wrong.

'You're quiet,' she said, genuinely concerned about her friend's lack of vitality.

Amanda's curls danced erratically round her heart-shaped face and she pushed them back for the umpteenth time.

'Sorry,' Sarah replied, 'I'm miles away today.'

'I can see that. What's up?'

Sarah sighed.

'Oh, I don't know. Nothing in particular, just tired.'

Amanda cocked her head to one side and raised an eyebrow.

'It's man trouble,' she announced, 'isn't it? Martin hasn't proposed to you, has he?'

Martin was Sarah's boss! He was a short man and was naturally concerned about his receding hair line at the tender age of thirty-six. He had a love of food which was speeding up the middle-age spread process considerably quicker than he desired. He was also quietly, but obviously, in love with Sarah. What he lacked in stature he made up for with charisma and business acumen.

Sarah liked him, and they often went out together for a meal or to see a show, but although they got on well the relationship was totally platonic as far as Sarah was concerned. Remembering the way her stomach had somersaulted yesterday when she was in the bookshop, secretly admiring the man with the red car, just went to confirm her feelings for Martin as merely brotherly. She wanted more, but not from him. Somebody was out there waiting for her, and she knew now that she regretted getting involved with Martin. Was it too late to back peddle without hurting him?

Sarah dabbed at the painting in front of her with a piece of lint then looked up at Amanda.

'No, it's not Martin, well, not directly. He's just stifling me, and I'm a bit frustrated with my life. I feel that I haven't done much and my job doesn't seem to be taking me anywhere. It's just not exciting enough. I want to know what I'll be doing ten years from now.'

'You are obviously having a mid-life crisis at the age of twenty-eight,' Amanda said, knowledgeably, 'or it could be post-Christmas blues.'

'In March?' Sarah queried. 'I think

it's more serious than that. I'll opt for the mid-life crisis. What is the cure?'

Amanda smiled.

'Why don't you come to Greece with me next month? It'll give you something to look forward to. All those lovely Greek waiters!'

'You asked me that two weeks ago,' Sarah reminded her.

'I know, and the offer still stands.'

'I'll let you know,' Sarah said. 'A holiday romance isn't on my agenda, though. I think I'm yearning for something a bit more permanent.'

'From the look of you, I'd say that you've already got your eye on someone, too!' Amanda said thoughtfully.

Sarah quickly shook a finger at Amanda.

'It's not Martin,' she stated, defensively.

'So you admit it is someone then?'

Amanda was suddenly more attentive, but before Sarah could confirm or deny, Martin breezed towards them.

''Morning ladies,' he greeted them.

‘‘Morning,’ they both replied in unison.

‘Your telephone is ringing Amanda,’ he said, and she reluctantly dashed off.

Martin turned his attention to Sarah.

‘You’re looking a bit down in the dumps today, my girl,’ he said affectionately. ‘Do you fancy coming out for a meal tonight?’ he added hopefully.

Sarah wondered if Amanda’s phone had really been ringing or had it been a ploy to send her scuttling off so he could speak to her?

‘I don’t think so, not tonight,’ Sarah declined. ‘I’ve been feeling tired these last few days. I ought to get an early night.’

Disappointed, Martin pulled a face.

‘Sure?’ he asked, irritating her now. ‘See how you feel later. Let me know if you change your mind.’

He patted her affectionately on the arm and Sarah sighed as he left the room. She really would have to say something to him and put things straight. He acted as though they were an item, and it was getting awkward now. She bent her head over her work and scrutinised the tear in the canvas.

To her relief, no one bothered her all morning and as she worked away on the old masterpiece her tensions began to fade. By one o'clock, she was feeling a bit better, at least she was hungry for lunch. She made her way quickly up to the attic staff room. Most of the staff were out or still working so there was only Amanda there, already making two mugs of tea in anticipation of Sarah's arrival.

'You look a bit more cheerful now,' Amanda remarked, seeing Sarah smile for the first time that day.

'I was in a bit of a funny mood this morning,' Sarah admitted.

'A funny mood!' Amanda said. 'I think suicidal mood would be nearer the description you are looking for,' she corrected and they both laughed.

Sarah took a swig of tea.

'Oh, that's better,' she said and drank it straight down.

Amanda watched her drain the mug.

'So, who is this man you've got your eye on?'

Sarah hesitated.

'Did I say there was one?' she answered cagily and moved across to the counter to flick on the kettle. 'More tea?'

'Yes, please,' Amanda replied, 'and stop avoiding my question. I know something has happened.'

Sarah stood by the window waiting for the kettle to boil again and looked down into the courtyard dreamily while she waited, ignoring Amanda's pleas for an answer. Her heart gave a little involuntary leap as her eyes came to rest on a red sports car parked below. It can't be the same one surely, she thought! That was too unlikely — until the dark man with the onyx ring emerged from Holberns Auctioneers office on the other side of the courtyard and she gave an audible gasp as she watched him walk over to his car.

'It's him!' she exclaimed, which

brought Amanda hurrying over to the window to see what was causing the stir.

'Who?' she asked and looked down at the man taking up all Sarah's attention. 'Wow! I knew there was a man involved. Come on, who is he?'

'I've no idea,' Sarah said, 'but I wish I knew,' and she quickly explained about their brief encounter the previous afternoon.

'He can have my parking place any time,' Amanda said, sighing as the car disappeared through the wrought iron gates into the London traffic.

That evening, Martin pulled a chair out for Sarah at Sardi's restaurant.

'I'm glad you changed your mind about coming out to dinner,' he said, the look on his face showing him to be more than just glad.

'I need to talk to you about something,' she replied, not sure at all how she was going to broach the subject.

Martin ignored the serious tone in

her voice and the solemn look on her face.

'I need to speak to you, too,' he said looking pleased with himself, and Sarah hoped he wasn't going to present her with an engagement ring. 'Let's order first.'

She wondered if it had been a bad idea after all accepting the dinner date, but she felt she owed him a proper explanation and somehow thought it would be easier in a public place. After all, she did enjoy his company and they did get on well together. She didn't want to destroy their friendship, she just didn't want the kind of relationship he hankered after and she was wearied fighting off his advances. She had to put a stop to it otherwise it would just amble on endlessly and she wouldn't be able to find what it was that she really wanted.

Their conversation was light as they waited for their starters to be served, then, as Sarah began to eat her pâté she glanced around the room. Her eyes were drawn to a man in the corner seated at a very intimate table for two in the shadows. Candlelight flickered romantically in the centre of the table casting strange shadows across his face.

Sarah's breath caught in her throat. She watched in disbelief at Mr Red Sports Car talking and laughing, and then her eyes fell upon the woman at whom his conversation was directed, seated right opposite him. She was sophisticated and well dressed, obviously tall, even though she was seated, with dark hair piled on top of her head and several escaped tendrils caressing her neck seductively. As she lifted her wine glass to her red lips she smiled across the table at her dinner companion, revealing perfect, straight white teeth.

Sarah thought she was very beautiful and was instantly jealous of this woman. She looked at her escort again, still surprised at seeing him again. It was almost as though he were following her around, teasing her. You should be with me, she thought longingly, then her eyes returned to Martin opposite her and she realised how unfairly she was treating him.

She felt numb for the rest of the evening, and could hardly eat her food, barely hearing a word Martin was saying to her. She was unable to say what she had to say to him, and kept glancing at the couple in the corner. She couldn't stop herself. Strange flutterings tickled her stomach. She felt as though she knew this man and resented the other woman holding his attention.

But who was he?

When the couple got up to leave, it hurt Sarah to see him put his hand on the woman's bare arm. Sarah imagined him touching her arm in a similar way and it sent a shiver up her spine.

'Are you all right?' Martin asked her. 'You haven't listened to a word I've been saying.'

'Sorry,' Sarah said. 'I'm miles away. It's just been a long day and I'm feeling quite exhausted.'

'I'm not boring you, am I?' he said.

'No of course not, Martin,' she lied. 'I've probably just had too much wine.'

Martin continued, 'I'm trying to talk to you about a business trip you might like, but I can see you're obviously not in the mood right now so we'll discuss it tomorrow morning and you can tell me what it was you wanted to talk to me about.'

He signalled to the waiter for the bill, which soon came on a saucer with some chocolate mints. He took the mints, handed them to Sarah and gave the saucer back to the waiter with his credit card on it.

Oh, hurry, Sarah thought, I just want to go home. Seeing the handsome stranger again had unsettled her, and she was disturbed by the fact that she couldn't blot him out of her mind.

Martin took Sarah's arm as they left the restaurant. The cold night air felt good on her flushed face. He led her to the car and opened the door for her and as she got in she sighed to herself. All that lay between her and sleep now was Martin persuading her to let him in for a nightcap. She really would have to make an excuse.

2

Sarah sat in Martin's office the next day nursing a cup of coffee wondering what this business trip was all about. He stood by the window.

'Right, well, it's about the Drayton collection which is going to be auctioned,' he began. 'Sir Hugh Drayton, as I told you last week, is a bit of an eccentric. The thing is, he won't have the paintings sent here. He wants me to send someone down to his country estate to clean them on site and prepare the auction at the manor. I don't know if he thinks we aren't capable of looking after his paintings. Personally I think he probably hasn't got them insured properly. They've been in the attic since before the First World War apparently.'

He paused to gauge Sarah's reaction.

'You want me to go?' she asked. 'To Cornwall?'

'Yes,' Martin confirmed. 'I wondered whether you'd consider it. He wants the best.'

Sarah blushed.

'Thank you, and I'd love to!' she said. 'I was gong to ask you for some time off, but working in Cornwall for a while in an old country house is ideal. Just what I need. What a wonderful opportunity.'

Martin was a little taken aback at her enthusiasm for getting away.

'Right then,' he said. 'Well, I'll ring him and confirm that then. Can you be ready to leave on Friday?'

'I'll make sure I am,' Sarah replied.

She couldn't wait to tell Amanda.

* * *

'You lucky thing!' Amanda said yet again as she sat on the edge of Sarah's bed watching her friend pack.

Sarah's usually tidy flat was in chaos.

'A paid trip to Cornwall, and staying

in a country house. I still can't believe your luck.'

'It's a working holiday,' Sarah corrected, 'and they are going to hold the auction there, too!'

Amanda was jealous.

'How come nothing like this ever happens to me?' she moaned.

Sarah just shrugged.

'You must be working in the wrong department.'

She held up a midnight-blue dress with delicate, spaghetti straps.

'Do you think I'll have to dress for dinner?' she asked.

'Well, that depends. You may just have to muck in and eat with the staff.'

'I hadn't thought of that,' Sarah admitted. 'Yes, of course, I'm not really a guest. I'll take it just in case though.'

She folded it carefully and laid it with the rest of the clothes she was taking.

'Are you taking a swimming costume?' Amanda asked.

'What for? I shan't be swimming in the sea in March,' Sarah stated. 'It's usually too cold in the middle of summer for me, let alone at this time of the year.'

'Just suppose they have a heated, indoor pool,' Amanda suggested.

Sarah paused and thought about that.

'All right, I'll take it, just in case.'

The telephone rang. Sarah hoped it wasn't Martin as Amanda lifted the receiver and spoke to the caller.

'Hello, oh, hello, Mrs Harper. No, it's Amanda. Sarah's here. Just a sec.'

She passed the receiver across the bed causing the rest of the phone to fall off the bedside table and dangle precariously while Sarah spoke to her mother.

'Hello, Mum, yes, I'm fine thanks, just packing now. Tomorrow afternoon.'

She answered her mother's questions patiently.

'Yes, Mum, you told me that yesterday. I will. Look, I have to go now. I'll call you later next week after I get there. Yes, 'bye.'

Amanda was giggling.

'What was all that about?'

'Don't ask,' Sarah winced. 'I'm sure Mum thinks I'm still a child. She phoned to remind me to take a hot water bottle with me!'

'Ah, bless her,' Amanda said, smiling. 'I do like your mum. She's really sweet.'

'You can borrow her while I'm away,' Sarah told her.

* * *

A peacock cried mournfully somewhere in the distance. Sarah opened the small, mullioned window in her room. She was sitting on the window seat, drinking her second cup of coffee from an exquisite bone china cup, looking out across the formal gardens. She hadn't seen a peacock since her arrival the previous day, but she had been told there were half a dozen or more in the grounds. Their melancholy cry seemed fitting around the austere grandness of Fontingray Manor. Haunting and sad, the house seemed to conceal a thousand secrets.

Sarah watched as an old man, bent with age, wheeled a barrow past the fountain. Under his cloth cap, she recognised Sam, the butler-cum-odd-job man who had greeted her on her arrival the previous evening. She had been rather startled by him at first, she recalled. Standing at the bottom of the steps she had looked up at the impressive main entrance admiring its columns and wealth of stone decoration. The double oak doors were carved with grotesque figures and entwined patterns of fruit and flowers, and the two stone lions on guard at either side of the steps had silently roared at her as one of the big doors had swung open to reveal the butler with an equally stony face peering down at her.

He was thickset with a very ruddy complexion and his eyes were almost completely concealed by shaggy grey eyebrows, but his stern countenance had cracked into a smile making him look less formidable as he had introduced himself and welcomed her to the manor. Then he had hobbled down the steps carefully to take her suitcase from the car. She had thought that the owners of the manor would have seen her that evening after her arrival but she was mistaken. Sam had shown her to her room and had some supper sent up, then given her directions to the great hall where Lady Isobel Drayton would see her in the morning, and that was that. She had stayed in her room until now.

She closed the window as a blast of cold air hit her face, reminding her that although the sun was shining, it was still a cold, March morning. She hugged her knees close to her body and felt a sense of excitement sweep over her as she anticipated the working holiday ahead in this lovely Elizabethan house. She looked around the room that was to be her temporary home for the next few weeks or so. It was old and slightly shabby-looking, but this only increased its enchanting atmosphere and timeless charm.

The four-poster bed was the most outstanding piece of furniture in the room, with carved bedsteads and dark rose-coloured curtains to keep out the draughts. The carving on the headboard depicted scenes of foreign lands and maritime adventure. It was a work of art in itself and Sarah marvelled at the amount of work that had been put into one item of furniture.

Sarah got up from her comfortable window niche and put the now-empty coffee cup down on the oak tray with the remains of her breakfast things. The breakfast tray had been brought to her room as had her supper the previous evening and she felt like a royal visitor. She was looking forward to meeting her hosts, Sir Hugh and Lady Isobel Drayton.

She sighed and stretched her limbs. For the first time in weeks she felt completely relaxed. She hadn't realised just how tense she had been. She'd been working very lard lately but now was looking forward to starting work in such lovely, peaceful surroundings. She would make sure that she got plenty of walks in, too, so she could really unwind and think long and hard about what she was going to do in the future.

She padded into the bathroom. Originally a dressing-room, it was now a mixture of Victorian furniture and modern plumbing which had been carefully added without the room losing its antique charm. The bath was of the old-fashioned kind with claw feet and the hand basin was set into an old Victorian washstand. Large, fluffy peach towels hung in brass rings along the wall and on a pine shelf above the bath was a selection of toiletries.

She turned on the bath taps. There was plenty of time for a bath. She selected some perfumed bubble bath and poured a little into the water. After a relaxing soak, she lifted the plug chain out with her toe and stood up reaching for a towel and dried herself vigorously.

Then she dressed quickly while thinking ahead with a new determination.

Life is what you make it, she told herself sternly, and decided this trip was going to be an adventure. She was thinking that over and over to herself as she left the room and stepped on to the landing, getting her bearings and trying to remember the directions Sam had given to her to get to the old hall where Isobel Drayton was going to meet her to discuss the work to be done.

The hall was large with a minstrels' gallery at the far end. Six tall, mullioned windows let in muted light and the walls were hung with heavy, dark tapestries, swords and various shields and coats of arms. On three sides of the room were numerous chairs and settles, and five winged settees with floral-patterned upholstery. Sarah could see all her boxes of paraphernalia and equipment on a long table covered with a baize cloth and propped up against the wall, her easel and lights ready to set up for work.

She had left her car keys with Sam, the butler, the previous evening and he had brought in all her equipment and then put her car away for her. She made her way to the table now.

She picked up her car keys and put them in her pocket, then busied herself with unpacking and getting comfortable in her surroundings. There was a faint scuffling noise above her in the minstrels' gallery and she took a few steps back to look up. It was dark, and she couldn't see much in the shadows, but she got the distinct impression that something or someone had been there. Now they had disappeared into thin air leaving Sarah with goosebumps. She shivered. Maybe it had been a car or just some creaking, she thought to herself.

She scolded herself for her vivid imagination but as she continued to sort out her equipment and unpack her brushes and bottles of solvent, she couldn't help but day-dream that her stay in this house was going to produce some kind of adventure and not be just the simple assignment that it appeared.

She looked at the pictures she was to clean. They were carefully propped up against the wall each draped with a dust sheet. Martin had told her they should fetch a fair price at the auction and Sarah wondered if the Draytons were strapped for cash.

She was examining one of them, a portrait of a small child with golden ringlets which the title declared was **Alice, 1728,** when a door opened and Isobel Drayton appeared. Sarah turned to see her hostess walking down the hall towards her.

'Good morning, Miss Harper,' Lady Isobel said brightly, extending her hand in greeting. 'Welcome to Fontingray. Thank you so much for agreeing to come down and do your work here at such short notice. I know it must seem a strange thing for you to have to go to the work rather than the paintings come to you, but my husband was very insistent, I'm afraid. He has his reasons.

I do hope you had a good journey.'

'Hello,' Sarah said, shaking the proffered hand. 'Yes, I did have a good journey. Thank you and the room is lovely. You have a wonderful house and please, call me Sarah.'

'Indeed, Sarah,' she replied. 'You must shout if you need anything.'

She was a tall woman in her early sixties, obviously very active, Sarah judged, from the way in which she had marched quickly down the hall. She wore no make-up except for a touch of pink lipstick, and was dressed casually.

'I'm almost ready to get started,' Sarah told her, indicating her tools.

'Oh, good, lovely. You can see the paintings which require your skills. Hugh will discuss the auction with you later when you've settled in.'

She inspected Sarah's tools and bottles on the table then walked over to the window and looked out across the wind-blown fields. Sarah joined her and followed Isobel's eyes out beyond the formal gardens.

'It looks like the weather is brightening up,' Isobel commented. 'You must get out while you are here and explore the grounds. We can't have you cooped up in here all day, can we?'

She smiled at Sarah, and took off her glasses, letting them dangle on the safety chain around her neck.

'I'll show you around the house later if you would like. It's steeped in history. We only live in part of the house now. The rest is very draughty and sadly crumbling around our ears.'

'That seems to add to its character,' Sarah replied. 'I adore old, unspoiled country houses. They have a timeless quality that can so easily be ruined by too much modernisation.'

'I agree with you, dear, but some things have to be done. With the money raised from the sale of these paintings we hope to be able to do some careful, much-needed restoration work on the place. The Drayton family has been here for over four hundred years, you know. I would hate to go down in history as the one who let the house crumble away.'

Just at that moment, a male figure came into view outside. He was striding across the large paved area that ran across the entire length of the building and Isobel and Sarah both watched him as he descended the steps from the terrace and set off purposefully in the direction of the old gatehouse, just visible beyond the trees.

He had some papers tucked under his arm, and Sarah watched incredulously as the very same man she had seen in London with the red car turned up the collar of the coat and bent his head against the wind. Her heart was thumping so loudly inside her chest that she felt sure Isobel would hear it. What on earth was he doing here? It was almost as though she kept conjuring him up from a dream. Isobel turned to Sarah.

'That's my son, Rhett. He's an author. He's written a series of fantasy fiction novels. You may have heard of him. He writes under the pseudonym of Maxwell Dunn.'

'Maxwell Dunn!' Sarah said in surprise. 'Why, yes, I have. He wrote *The Amarin Chronicles*, didn't he? I haven't read them myself, but my brother, James, is an ardent fan. Well, fancy that.'

She was finding it hard to believe the coincidence. It was just too unlikely, but it did explain his presence at Holberns Auctioneers the previous week, He was probably arranging her visit and the coming auction of the Drayton Collection.

Isobel smiled proudly, but her smile disappeared as quickly as it had appeared.

'He's becoming very successful with his writing. He has put all his energies into it since his wife died two years ago.'

Sarah looked at Isobel curiously. There was a pause as though her host was contemplating whether or not to confide in Sarah, then she continued, 'She died tragically in childbirth. It was very sad. Not something you expect might happen in modern times.'

'Oh, how dreadful,' Sarah said, her sympathy flying out to him immediately.

'It was, it was,' Isobel said sadly. 'It affected him quite deeply — well, all of us, really. They both used to live here in the big house, with Hugh and me, but afterwards, Rhett moved into the gatehouse. He said he found it easier to write down there. I expect that's true, but he doesn't like to be reminded of Bridie, and of course with little Harry and his nanny living here, it's a constant reminder.'

She stared wistfully at Rhett's figure moving through the trees towards his retreat and sighed. She had almost forgotten Sarah standing beside her. Sarah was a little embarrassed about Isobel confiding personal family tragedies to her, and stood silently, unsure what to do next, until Isobel snapped back to the present.

'Look, I mustn't interrupt you any

longer. You must be anxious to get started. I'll leave you for now. Beth will bring you some coffee in a minute and lunch is at one o'clock. Beth is our cook-cum-housekeeper. Later this afternoon I'll show you round the house. Will that be all right?'

'That will be fine,' Sarah assured her. 'I'll look forward to my tour immensely.'

Isobel was pleased and retreated to the door, but with her hand resting on the door knob she turned to Sarah again.

'If you do need anything, there's a ring cord next to the fireplace. One pull will bring Beth or her assistant, Lucy.'

'Thank you,' Sarah said and then Isobel was gone, leaving Sarah alone in the old hall.

3

Sarah looked up at the portraits of Drayton ancestors staring out of their huge gilt frames in an eternal vigil. Isobel, a few steps ahead of her on the staircase was talking to her non-stop about the history of Fontingray. She had told Sarah that they didn't have many visitors and she was obviously revelling in her rôle as guide. Sarah was pleased to listen. It was her favourite subject after all.

Isobel pointed up to a painting of a dark, swarthy-looking man with a black pointed beard who was staring coldly out of his flat, painted world.

'This is Fabian Drayton, who was Earl here in 1640. My grandfather, who was an historian, wrote about him in one of his books which is in the library. Fabian was the Bluebeard of the family.'

Sarah shivered and Isobel saw she had her undivided attention and continued.

'He was reputed to have been a wrecker along the treacherous coast hereabouts. Apparently, so the story goes, after one particularly bad storm, a Spanish sailor was washed ashore from a stricken ship. Fabian's wife, Aramantha, secretly rescued him and hid him while she nursed him back to health, but she fell in love with him and when, eventually, Fabian found out, he poisoned them both and bricked them up together in a room in the east wing.'

'How dreadful,' Sarah interjected.

Isobel was really enjoying herself.

'A bricked-up room was discovered in 1937 and it contained two skeletons, a man and a woman. They are in the museum in Castleford, a few miles away.'

Sarah was quite moved.

'What a romantic and tragic tale,' she declared, 'but just how true is it? I mean I thought wrecking was just a

Cornish legend not a genuine ancient occupation.'

'Well,' Isobel continued authoritatively, 'there actually isn't a lot of concrete evidence that induced wrecking took place. It has been said that the wreckers used to attach lamps to wandering cliff-top cows and their meandering looked like another ship's lights wallowing in swelling seas, giving sailors a false sense of direction and sometimes causing accidental grounding on the rocks, but the actual sport of ship plundering was much more real. You see there was a frequency of disasters anyway, mainly due to inaccurate charts, over-laden, undermanned ships, strong currents and such and this meant that many ships floundered on the rocks without any interference from someone on the cliffs. Navigational aids were very hit and miss and many ship masters couldn't use a sextant properly.'

There was no stopping Isobel now, Sarah realised.

'If there were no survivors then the ship was officially a wreck and salvage was legitimate. Whole villages used to follow a ship in distress with wheelbarrows and carts just waiting for it to go aground then they'd be on to it like vultures. The actual crime was not trying to save any lives, because if there were survivors, the ship could not legally be claimed as salvage.

'May I see the room that was bricked up?' Sarah asked, morbid fascination encouraging her curiosity.

'Of course. It's in the east wing, the part in most disrepair, but I'll show you the rooms in this wing first. These are the ones we are able to look after.'

They toured the west wing and Sarah was enchanted by everything she saw. Isobel knew so much about the history of the house. She loved it dearly and seemed very content to impart her knowledge to Sarah. She followed Isobel dutifully through the Blue Room, the Chinese Room, the Music Room, library, studio, study and numerous bedrooms, ante-chambers and corridors.

A lot of the furniture was shrouded in dust sheets for protection and shutters were closed to keep out the sunlight that would fade delicate fabrics.

'It is such a shame that it has to be left like this,' Isobel confided to Sarah. 'If we could afford it, we would be able to restore it all and preserve it all properly and open it to the public.'

'A mammoth task,' Sarah agreed, 'but a wonderful, worthwhile project. I would love to be involved with something like that. You are very lucky to have all this.'

Isobel had her hand on a rope rail at the bottom of a winding, stone staircase.

'I wish everyone felt as you do, dear,' she said. 'I can tell you have a love of history, and it is lovely to show someone around who appreciates the inner beauty here. Hugh just calls it a millstone round his neck and Rhett doesn't even see it at all.'

'Such a shame,' Sarah commented. 'The place has so many possibilities. Mediaeval jousts, banquets, falconry, archery . . . '

'You see it exactly as I do,' Isobel said enthusiastically. 'I have so many ideas. I'd open the house and gardens, have tea-rooms and a gift shop. I even thought of converting the stable block into little units for cottage industries.'

'Oh, yes,' Sarah said. 'You could have a potter's wheel churning out pottery, then there's lace-making, needlepoint, picture framing. I wouldn't mind a little shop like that myself. When you've done it all I'll come down and rent one from you.'

Isobel sighed.

'It's just so refreshing to find someone on the same wavelength. I don't expect, though, that there will be much money left after the sale of the paintings once we have sorted out the roof and the dry rot. I do feel that we have a duty to look after our heritage, especially for Harry's sake. Come, this staircase leads to the attic rooms which used to house the schoolroom and nursery.'

She went ahead up the stone steps, round and round until Sarah thought she would keel over from being dizzy, but they reached the top without such embarrassment. Sarah thought she could hear the laughter of past Drayton children coming from behind the large, oak door that confronted them on the small landing they had arrived on but the voices faded as Isobel pushed open the door.

The old school desks stood silent and heavy with dust and memories. It made Sarah feel sad and in the abandoned nursery the melancholy feeling was stronger and she was certain that she saw the moth-eaten rocking-horse move. She imagined the room busy with children playing while the elder children were tutored next door.

'It's haunting,' she said to Isobel.

'I wish Hugh and Rhett found it so,'

she repeated. 'Even if we had the money it wouldn't be something I could tackle alone.'

Sarah was lost in a daydream for a few moments, thinking about herself and Rhett tackling the restoration together.

'Maybe he is still grieving,' she said.

Isobel frowned and Sarah was conscious of the fact that she had spoken the words aloud.

'Rhett, I mean,' she said. 'Maybe he is still grieving for his wife. You couldn't expect him to take on such a project if he was unhappy.'

'No, you're right,' Isobel agreed, 'but . . . well . . . for Harry . . . '

They were both silent for a moment. Then Isobel took a deep breath.

'I've taken up enough of your time, Sarah. Let me show you the room where Aramantha and her sailor were entombed. Then you can get on with your work. Beth will be bringing you afternoon tea soon and she will wonder where you are. Oh, I nearly forgot. Will you have dinner with us tonight, me, Hugh and Rhett?'

Later that afternoon, when Sarah had finished for the day, she made her way to the library to borrow some books at Isobel's invitation. The room where Aramantha and her sailor had been locked up had been a disappointment to her. Even knowing that their remains were housed in Castleford museum, Sarah had at least expected some signs of their occupation. Instead, it just looked like all the other bedrooms Isobel had taken her through. She wondered if she would find some interesting books on the subject to quell her disappointment.

She pushed open the library door and slipped inside, only to be stopped dead in her tracks. Rhett was sitting in a chair at the far end of the room poring over the yellowing pages of a very ancient-looking tome on the desk in front of him.

Since that time last week in Samson's Bookshop, and the realisation that he was just the type of man she had been looking for all her life, she had conjured up his features in all her daydreams. Now seeing him so close, she saw that he was exactly as she had recalled him. She had even conjured up the smell of the after-shave he had worn. She wouldn't forget it in a hurry. She felt giddy and excited.

Rhett swung round in his chair at the sound of Sarah's footsteps and threw her completely off her guard. She felt her cheeks begin to glow alarmingly and her mouth went dry. Then she lost the art of speech! She tried smiling but Rhett's face remained unchanged apart from the vague look of bewilderment at the intrusion. Sarah found her voice at last.

'Oh, sorry,' she squeaked. 'I didn't realise anyone was in here.'

'Anyone?' he queried. 'I'm not anyone. I live here. Who are you?'

She walked forward and held out her hand.

'Sarah Harper, from Holberns. I'm

cleaning the paintings for the auction next month. You must be Rhett Drayton. I saw you at Holberns last week.'

Rhett ignored her hand. It dangled there awkwardly and Sarah was acutely aware that he had done that on purpose.

Please don't do this to me, she thought to herself. I really want you to be nice to me.

Rhett looked her up and down as if gauging her reaction to his brusque manner. A test?

'Oh, yes,' he said, 'it was mentioned. For some reason I was expecting a man.'

Her hackles rose.

'I'm fully qualified,' she retorted.

'You wouldn't be here if you weren't,' he assured her.

The conversation was going badly, not like in her daydreams, where she was in control and he was falling in love with her.

She hunted for something intelligent to say to bring the conversation back to friendly introduction.

'Isobel said I could borrow some books while I am here, but I can see you're busy. I'll come back later.'

'No, no, that's OK,' Rhett insisted, standing up.

Sarah relaxed.

'My concentration's gone now anyway. I'll get my things and leave you to it.'

Sarah tensed again, and wished she didn't find him so attractive.

'My fault,' she admitted and apologised again for intruding.

There was no reply.

'You live in the gate-house, don't you?' she asked.

Awkward silence.

'How's the book going?'

Rhett raised one eyebrow and looked at her suspiciously.

'For someone who's been here less than twenty-four hours, you seem to know rather a lot about me.'

'Your mother very kindly gave me a guided tour of the house earlier and she did talk about its occupants, too, hence the library visit. She told me about Aramantha and the Spanish sailor. Whetted my appetite for ancient legends.'

Rhett laughed and Sarah laughed, too. His eyes crinkled at the corners and his mouth softened. He wasn't so stern looking now. Sarah felt in control again.

'I thought there may be some books on the subject.'

She hoped he would offer to help her look for some.

'I daresay there are,' he said and began collecting his papers together. 'I'm sure you'll find some.'

He began moving towards the door. Sarah saw she was in danger of losing him before they'd had a proper conversation.

'I've been invited to dinner tonight,' she said lamely. 'You'll be there, too, won't you?'

He pretended to ponder the question for a moment.

'Do you want me to be?' he asked.

'It might be interesting,' Sarah replied nonchalantly.

Rhett laughed.

'I'll think about it. You remind me of someone. Have we met before?'

Sarah smiled.

'I'll tell you later.'

Rhett managed to look intrigued as he disappeared and Sarah was left feeling slightly more hopeful but still wondering if he had been attempting to tease her or was just being naturally rude and sarcastic.

4

The telephone had rung more than several times and still Amanda hadn't answered it. Sarah thought she may have gone out. It was Saturday night after all. She was just about to switch off her mobile, when it clicked into life.

'Hello,' Amanda's perky little voice came.

'Amanda, it's me, Sarah.'

'Oh, hi. How's it going? You got there all right then?'

'Yes,' Sarah replied, 'and you'll never guess.'

She was never one for holding back when she had something she was dying to tell her friend.

'What?' Amanda asked, excitedly.

'My man in the red sports car? Well, you won't believe this, but by the most amazing coincidence, he lives right here in Fontingray Manor. He's the Draytons' son, Rhett. He's a writer and I've just met him this afternoon.'

'Slow down, slow down. You are joking,' Amanda said incredulously, then, 'Tell me all, at once!' she demanded.

So Sarah willingly related the events of the day and then the conversation which she had had with Rhett in the library, word for word. When she had finished giving Amanda all the details, the two of them began to put connotations on every angle of the conversation.

'Are you sure he wasn't just being ill-mannered?' Amanda asked.

'Well, fairly sure,' Sarah answered. 'I mean, I think he was aiming to tease and it came out wrong, or maybe he was just being cautious. He had a definite look in his eyes that said he was attracted to me. I saw it. Not only that, earlier today in the Old Hall where I am working, I felt certain that I was being watched. And it wasn't just by the suits of armour. I think he was up in the minstrels' gallery spying on me, checking me out.'

'He may have been checking to see if you were working, doing your job properly,' Amanda observed. 'Did you tell him that you saw him in London, and drooled all over him from the upstairs window of Holberns last week?'

'No, I didn't,' Sarah admitted. 'Plenty of time for all that. For the moment I am convinced that he likes what he sees though.'

'If he doesn't turn up for dinner tonight, you'll know you were wrong.'

'I hope not.' Sarah sighed. 'There's something about him which really intrigues me. Anyway, look, I've got to finish getting ready. I'll ring you again and let you know what's happening.'

'You'd better,' Amanda said. 'I want all the details. Have a nice evening. I'll talk to you later.'

'Yes, 'bye then.'

Sarah switched off the phone and contemplated the evening ahead. She tried not to think about the suggestion that Amanda had made — that Rhett might decide not to turn up. This might be the only time she would be invited to dine with Lord and Lady Drayton. If her future meals were to be taken quietly by herself or with the other staff, then she intended to make the most of this evening, and she just hoped that Rhett was curious enough to want to see her again.

Her stomach was doing somersaults as she thought about him while she applied her make-up. She hoped that her yearning for romance and adventure had not loosened her grip on reality. She looked at her reflection in the floor-length mirror and decided that she was dressed a little over the top in the midnight-blue dress that Amanda had talked her into taking with her just in case. But she hadn't really anything else suitable, and besides, if Rhett did make an appearance she aimed to make the most of it.

She added a subtle spray of her

favourite perfume, then paused before she opened the door to face the evening. She was idly wondering if Rhett was in a relationship at the moment as she remembered the woman he had been dining with in London the evening she had been out with Martin. Who was she? Someone important to him? They had certainly seemed to be getting on well with each other.

She left her room and walked slowly and sedately down the main staircase. The lights were low and cast strange shadows. At the bottom she turned to the right and made her way towards the dining-room. The door was ajar and the lights inside, brighter, were beckoning. She could hear talking, recognising Isobel Drayton's soft, dulcet tones and then a man's voice she hadn't heard before, probably Sir Hugh, she thought.

She knocked gently and pushed the door open, stepping inside. She had seen this room earlier when Isobel had shown her around. It had been dark and shadowy, but now it was alive and splendid. Fresh flowers adorned the centre of the table and silver candelabra graced each end. The table was laid with silver cutlery and crystal glasses and Sarah wondered how often, if ever, they went to these lengths at dinner.

Sir Hugh and Lady Isobel were standing by one of the many side tables, drinking sherry. Isobel, on hearing Sarah's entrance, immediately went to greet her.

'Sarah, my dear, you look stunning,' she declared. 'Do come and join us for a sherry.'

'Thank you,' Sarah replied, following her to the table, feeling like an honoured guest rather than the temporary resident restorer.

Isobel laid a hand on her husband's jacket.

'Hugh, dear, this is Sarah Harper. Sarah, my husband, Hugh.'

Sarah shook hands with Hugh Drayton.

'Very nice to meet you, sir,' she said, unsure how to address him.

'And you, Sarah, and you. I've been looking at the work you've achieved today. Splendid start. Martin Copeman at Holberns said you were highly skilled at your job and very dedicated.'

'Well, thank you, sir. It is nice to be appreciated.'

'Call me Hugh,' he insisted. 'I'm very grateful that you were able to come down at such short notice. I hope we haven't dragged you away from your family.'

'No, you haven't,' Sarah assured him. 'I live on my own. No one will miss me.'

Martin's face appeared in her mind and she quickly pushed it away.

'On your own.' Hugh feigned surprise. 'A pretty thing like you?'

Isobel handed Sarah a glass of sherry and scolded her husband mildly.

'Don't embarrass the poor girl,' she said, and picked her glass up from the table and chinked it with Sarah's. 'Cheers,' she said. 'I hope you enjoy your stay with us and I hope the auction goes well and we get good prices for the paintings.'

'I will love it here,' Sarah returned, 'and I've every reason to think the auction will go without a hitch. The paintings are very interesting. They may be old and dirty but they are in remarkable condition.'

'That's no way to speak about my parents,' a voice joked from the doorway and Rhett strode in, immediately filling the room with his presence and causing Sarah's knees to buckle.

'You can stop teasing, too,' Isobel chided, but she was smiling and Sarah's cheeks started to redden.

It always infuriated her that it was the one thing about herself that she couldn't control. Rhett moved across the room and gave his mother a perfunctory kiss on the cheek and his father a nod.

'Good evening.'

He greeted everyone and picked up a glass of sherry. Sarah's heart was missing beats again as she tried to stop herself staring at the man in front of her with the flashing eyes and devil-may-care attitude.

'Rhett, this is Sarah Harper, the restorer from Holberns,' Lady Isobel introduced and Sarah held out her hand to him for the second time that day.

She eyed him nervously, but this time he took her hand and shook it warmly. The touch of his hand sent sparks to every nerve and she stopped herself from gasping, but couldn't do anything about the involuntary shiver his touch had triggered.

'Nice to see you, again,' he added, then to his mother, 'We met each other in the library earlier.'

Bravely Sarah interjected.

'Actually, we've met before today.'

Sir Hugh slurped his sherry noisily, but Isobel looked at Sarah for an explanation. Rhett frowned at her.

'I said that I thought you seemed familiar,' he admitted.

'Last week, in Central London,'

Sarah began. 'I very unfairly accused you of stealing my parking space and you quite rightly criticised my driving skills.'

He thought for a moment, and smiled as realisation dawned on him.

'I remember now. I just couldn't place you. Yes, that was it. Did you get a ticket from that traffic warden?'

'I missed it by the skin of my teeth,' Sarah admitted, beginning to relax with him.

'Fancy that,' Isobel said. 'Rhett hardly ever goes up to London.'

Another door opened just then and wheels clacked heralding the arrival of the dinner trolley guided by the expert driving skills of Beth, the cook.

'Dinner is served, ma'am,' she announced, and Isobel requested everyone to be seated, steering Sarah to a seat directly opposite Rhett.

Beth served them all with a fresh mushroom soup and tiny rolls which she had baked herself. Sarah ate and answered Sir Hugh's and Lady Isobel's questions as she surveyed Rhett from beneath her eyelashes, pleased to notice he was doing the same to her.

'How long have you been doing this restoration stuff then?' Sir Hugh asked.

'Six years now,' Sarah replied. Then added for Rhett's benefit, 'I really love the job, but I must admit I'm not keen on living in London and I want to expand from just working on paintings. I want to get involved with restoring fabrics, wall coverings, clothing, that kind of thing. I am waiting for the chance to move away and get involved with a big restoration project.'

Sir Hugh laughed.

'We've got one of those right here ourselves, and we don't want it.'

'Yes, we do, dear,' Isobel told him. 'Now don't speak like that. Sarah will think you don't like the place.'

'It's a millstone around our necks and you know it,' Sir Hugh mumbled into his soup. 'Has Isobel shown you round the place yet? She loves practising her guide skills.'

Sarah smiled.

'Yes, we went over it this afternoon. It's a wonderful house and I agree restoration would certainly be a massive project.'

Isobel nodded.

'Yes, and the problem needs addressing sooner rather than later.'

'There you go again, dear,' Hugh said and looked at his wife appealingly. 'We're getting the roof seen to, and the dry rot at least. It's a start.'

'I know,' she said, 'but I would like to restore the whole place and get it opened to the public.'

'It's a lovely idea, even though it's ambitious,' Sarah agreed and noticed that Rhett was looking at her strangely.

'Count me out,' he said, holding up his hands. 'I'm much too busy with my writing.'

'You should be thinking about it, Rhett,' his mother added, 'for Harry's sake.'

'Don't start, Mother,' Rhett replied tersely and Sarah could see they were approaching dangerous ground.

'Your writing, yes,' she said, showing interest. 'Tell me about it. What made you want to be a writer? I mean, it's a very lonely occupation.'

'I'm a very lonely man,' he replied.

'You don't have to be.'

Sarah looked into his eyes, but they told her nothing.

'Perhaps I want to be,' he said, almost snappily.

'You're going to end up just like your father if you're not careful,' Isobel warned him.

'What's that supposed to mean?' Hugh said indignantly.

'Well, you spend all day in your workshop carving wooden birds while the place falls down around our ears, and Rhett gets just as involved with his writing.'

Isobel turned to look at Sarah.

'Sometimes we don't see Rhett for days on end, especially if he's in one of his write-all-night, sleep-all-day moods.'

Sarah looked at him again.

'You want to be careful you don't change into a bat,' she joked.

'If I find myself hanging up-side down in the wardrobe, I'll heed your warning.'

It was almost sarcastic, the way he said it.

By the time the main course had been cleared away and they were eating fresh fruit salad with Cornish clotted cream the conversation had become much lighter and Sarah had managed to make Rhett laugh several times with her wit. She really wanted to ask him about himself though and his little boy, Harry, but she knew she couldn't, especially not in front of Hugh and Isobel.

After a few more glasses of wine Rhett did loosen up a bit and even divulged the plot of his latest book although his attitude had cooled. He seemed guarded, but even though the conversation was a little stilted, by the time coffee was served Sarah had fallen head-over-heels for him and knew that she could never go back to London and carry on as before!

As soon as he had drunk his coffee, Rhett stood up and announced his intention to retire and leave them to it.

'So early, dear?' Isobel commented.

Rhett looked at the clock. It was just ten thirty.

Not exactly a party animal, Sarah thought, disappointed that the evening was to end so abruptly.

'I hope you continue to enjoy your stay here, Sarah,' he said as he pushed back his chair and stood up.

She forced a smile at Rhett as he bade her good-night and left the room.

'Oh, well, more coffee, Sarah?' Isobel said.

Sarah would have preferred just to go to her room and dream of how the evening could have ended, but good manners forced her to accept more coffee and carry on chatting the evening away.

The evening hadn't exactly worked out the way Sarah had anticipated.

Rhett's departure had seemed very dismissive, as though he had no intentions of seeing her again before she left. She had been relieved to reach the sanctuary of her room. She went and stared out of her window across to the gatehouse and saw that the upstairs lights were still on.

Was Rhett having trouble sleeping, as she knew she would? Or was he beginning an all-night writing session with all thoughts of her gone from his mind while he wrestled with fantasy characters from his own imaginary world?

Her heart sunk deeper as she contemplated the very real possibility of not seeing him again for the remainder of her stay. What excuse could she think of for visiting him? If she interrupted him when he was busy writing, she knew he wouldn't welcome the intrusion at all. It was with a heavy heart and a sense of failure that she crawled into the four-poster bed that night and it was several hours before she drifted off into a fretful, restless sleep.

5

Work was far from easy the next morning. Sarah had a headache from drinking too much wine and the Old Hall was cold and uninviting with no sun pouring through the high, leaded windows. Dark clouds had rolled in from the east and the wind was getting up. It whistled round the chimney and blew in all the cracks. The windows rattled and made Sarah feel uneasy.

She struggled hard to concentrate and it was several hours before she managed to dispel all the cobwebs and shake herself awake. By noon the weather calmed slightly and a weak, watery sun attempted to shine.

Sarah put down her tools and stretched, deciding to have a break and go down to the kitchen instead of waiting for Beth to bring her up some sandwiches.

Outside the Old Hall, over in the corner, a narrow staircase led down to the kitchens by way of a long, low-ceilinged, flag-stoned corridor. Sarah followed the sounds of chinking and clanking until she stooped under a beam at the end of the corridor and went down three steps into the original kitchens.

Beth looked up as Sarah descended the steps.

'Hello, my love,' the cook greeted her. 'Are you feeling a bit peckish already?'

'A bit,' Sarah replied. 'I thought I'd have a change of scenery. You don't mind, do you?'

'Not at all, love. We don't have enough guests down here,' Beth replied. 'Come and sit yourself down.'

She directed Sarah to a pine side table and pulled a chair out for her.

'I've got some pasties not long out of the oven. Do you fancy one of them?'

'That sounds lovely. I could smell them as I came along the corridor.'

Beth placed one in front of her with a large knob of butter melting over the top and handed her a knife and fork. As Sarah tucked in hungrily Beth busied herself making a pot of tea for them both.

'You live in London then,' she said while she warmed the pot.

'Mm. This is delicious.'

'You'll find it a bit quiet down here in the country. Nothing much doing round here. It must be all go up in the big city.'

'It is,' Sarah agreed. 'I must admit I don't really enjoy it any more. It's too hectic. I would really love to live down this way with all this fresh air, peace and tranquillity.'

'I've never been farther north than Exeter,' Beth announced proudly, as though it was some kind of great feat. 'Have you been for a walk around the grounds yet, or down to the beach?' she added.

Sarah shook her head as she continued eating.

'I would have gone out this morning, but the weather was dreadful.'

'It's looking brighter now though,' Beth informed her.

She was packing a basket with home-made bread, a slab of creamy yellow cheese, a fruit cake and pasties wrapped in crisp white tea-cloths. She saw Sarah watching her curiously.

'I'm taking this over to the gatehouse in a minute for Mr Rhett. He doesn't eat properly.'

Sarah's interest was roused.

'I'll come with you, if that's all right,' she offered, carefully keeping her voice on an even keel. 'I could do with some fresh air.'

'Yes, do, that's fine.'

Beth had no reason to suspect Sarah's real motive — to get closer to the gatehouse, to Rhett.

Lucy, Beth's young helper, entered the kitchen from a door at the other end of the room, carrying potatoes and carrots. Sarah had finished eating and was standing up.

'Hello,' Lucy said.

'This is Sarah, from London. She's here cleaning Lord Drayton's pictures for the auction,' Beth introduced her.

'Hello,' Sarah said.

Lucy plonked the vegetables down on the large, central work table. She flicked her hair back and pulled up her sleeves.

'I saw you arrive the other night,' she stated. 'I was cycling down the driveway as you came up. How long are you here for?'

'A couple of weeks,' Sarah told her.

Beth had her coat on and was picking up the basket.

'We're just off for a walk,' she informed Lucy. 'You can get on with those vegetables while I'm gone.'

Sarah fetched her jacket and met Beth outside. The sun was still shining, doing its best to warm everything up but it was a feeble attempt. The air was still cold and wintry and every now and then a short gust of wind blew around the pair as they walked across the corner of the main terrace and down some steps to join the path that led through the formal gardens towards the trees.

'How long have you worked for the Draytons?' Sarah asked.

'Oh, quite a few years,' Beth replied, trying to recall how many exactly. 'It feels like a hundred sometimes. Sam was estate manager here back in the Sixties. I met him when I was nineteen. He was twenty-eight and we got married the following year. He'd been living in an old cottage on the estate, down by the river, but it was in a terrible state, so they let us move in above the old coach house and I worked in the house for Lady Drayton.'

'You must have known Rhett when he was quite young then,' Sarah said.

'Oh, yes, love. He would have been about three years old then I suppose, a dear little boy. I remember he always used to come to me for a plaster when he scraped his knee, and one of my saffron buns. When the old cook died, I took on the rôle of cook/housekeeper and it's stayed that way ever since, except I've got Lucy now to help. Of course Sam doesn't run the estate anymore. It got too much for him. They've got a new manager now. But Sam's quite happy just pottering around the gardens, and seeing to odd jobs in the house.'

Sarah didn't really want to talk about Sam — she was much more interested in Rhett, so when a tall girl with the red hair came into view walking away from them across the other side of the gardens, hand in hand with a small boy, Sarah saw the opportunity to divert the conversation back to Rhett.

'That must be Harry with his nanny. I expected her to be older for some reason.'

'Coleen Brooks,' Beth informed her. 'She's not very old, no, I grant you, twenty-four I believe, but she's a trained nursery-nurse and apparently very good. I don't like her very much myself. She's very good with Harry but, well, I find her a bit strange, and sometimes I get the distinct impression that she'd much rather be somewhere else other than living quietly here with a little lad.'

'It must have been hard for everyone here when Rhett's wife died. Lady Isobel must have been grateful for Coleen's help.'

If Sarah's questioning seemed nosey and her interest in Rhett more than simple curiosity, Beth didn't notice. Luckily for Sarah the cook loved gossiping and was only too pleased to impart whatever information Sarah requested.

'Oh, it was awful,' Beth recalled, 'simply dreadful. So unexpected and tragic. Rhett was beside himself with grief. Lady Isobel had to see to the baby. But the worse thing is that Rhett seems to want nothing to do with little Harry. He doesn't want to be reminded of Bridie at all, so the poor little lad spends all day with that strange girl when he should be with his family. It's criminal really, but that's not for me to say.'

'How long were they married?' Sarah continued.

'Not long at all,' Beth replied with a shake of her head. 'Bridie had been running her own antique shop in London when they first got together. Then she suddenly sold up and came down here. They married and a year later she was dead. She'd had such plans for this place, too.'

'That's really sad,' Sarah agreed, thinking, no wonder Rhett wasn't interested in restoring the house, and with her chattering on about it over dinner, it must have sounded like history repeating itself.

They were approaching the trees and Sarah could see the gatehouse looming up in front of them. Red-bricked and imposing with what looked like far too many chimneys for such a small house, it was surrounded on three sides by black railings which, as far as Sarah could see, served no purpose at all.

'Rhett used to live in the main house,

didn't he?' Sarah prompted.

'Yes,' Beth told her. 'He and Bridie had a suite of rooms above the Old Hall where you are working. After she died he spent most of his time writing down at the gatehouse and then he moved in permanently. It's in an awful state of disrepair though. He can't possibly be comfortable. No one has occupied it for years and on the far side you can even see where part of the roof is missing. He's crazy.'

'People do crazy things when they are grieving,' Sarah added, remembering that he didn't seem to be doing much grieving when she saw him in the restaurant with that woman last week.

'It's been two years now. He's still young. It's not healthy to stay in mourning for ever. He should be trying to forget, be out meeting people. You know, finding someone to be with, to be a new mum to Harry.'

'He doesn't have a girlfriend then?' Sarah commented innocently.

'Not that I've seen,' Beth replied.

Beth pushed open the black wrought-iron gate that dangled on one rusty hinge. It squeaked and Sarah looked up above her at the empty dark windows wondering if anyone was watching their approach from the shadows. They walked silently up the overgrown path, and under the rotting, green-painted porch.

Sarah stood behind Beth in the small covered area that was open to the elements. The ground was littered with a carpet of twigs and leaves. Some had been blown up into a pile in the corner. Beth opened the rusty latch and pushed the door open.

'Anyone home?' she called out.

No reply, so she stepped over the threshold.

'Hello? Rhett? I've brought you some bits of baking, love.'

Silence screamed back at them. Sarah had joined Beth inside the very bleak-looking, old scullery. It was basic by anyone's standards and very untidy. Sarah was pleased to note no woman's touch was evident. There were empty mugs stacked on the table and an abundance of empty wine bottles. Several days' worth of plates were stacked up on the draining board.

Beth moved towards the table and made some room for the basket. There wasn't a sound from the house at all, not even a ticking clock. Sarah wondered if Rhett was writing somewhere in the house, ignoring Beth's calls, not wanting to be disturbed. Or was he out, even up at the main house maybe, in the library?

She half expected a noise behind her to reveal his presence but there was nothing. Beth picked up an empty basket from a previous visit and indicated to Sarah that their errand was completed. Sarah tried not to look disappointed as they retraced their steps and began to make their way back to the house.

6

Ignoring the cold, Sarah had walked around the formal gardens twice, deep in her thoughts. She was contemplating walking to the beach when she saw Beth emerge from one of the side doors carrying another of her baskets, no doubt full of her baking again. She certainly spoiled Rhett Drayton. Without hesitation she hurried towards the cook with one idea in her mind.

'Is that for Rhett? Can I take it for you?' she asked as she caught up with Beth. 'I'm on my way to the beach for a walk. I can drop it off at the gatehouse on my way past.'

Several days had passed by, quietly and uneventfully since their first visit to the gatehouse together. Sarah had been working long and hard on the paintings during the day, taking her meals quietly in the kitchen and spending the evenings reading books from the Fontingray library. Her working days had been interrupted only by Isobel, for the occasional chat, and Hugh to oversee the progress of his paintings. Sadly there had been no appearance by Rhett and Sarah saw the basket errand as her ideal opportunity to see him again. She was sure a push in the right direction was all that was needed to strike up a friendship between them.

'Yes, it is for Brett,' Beth said gratefully. 'Oh, that would be a help, love. I've got some estate workers turning up for pasties shortly. I don't know where the morning's gone.'

She thrust the basket into Sarah's hands.

'Are you sure it's no trouble?'

'Quite sure,' Sarah said and smiled, knowingly, as she watched Beth retreat the way she had just come.

Armed with her perfect excuse, Sarah strolled along the paths that Beth had taken her down before. The gatehouse soon loomed in front of her. She pushed open the familiar broken gate and trod the lichen-covered pathway up to the back porch. It was only as she reached to knock at the door that she began to feel a little nervous.

She waited several moments and knocked two or three more times, but there was no response, just like before, so she lifted the latch and pushed the door open, just enough to poke her head round and check the scullery for occupants. It was much as it had been before when she had come with Beth, except that there were a few more mugs on the table and the stack of plates on the drainer was an inch or two higher. Sarah stepped right in and surveyed the mess.

'Hello!' she called out. 'Anyone home?'

It was like a replay of her previous visit. Silence. Was no one home?

Another empty basket sat abandoned on a wooden stool though, at least proof that there had been some signs of life there over the last few days. Sarah placed the full basket on the table and picked up the empty one. There was a doorway on the far side of the scullery leading to the rest of the house. It beckoned to her and she had put down the basket and was through it before she could stop herself!

It led to a dark, inner hallway with two doors and a staircase leading off it. She looked in the rooms. One was a bathroom, very male orientated, full of navy towels and with that distinct smell of aftershave that Sarah would recognise anywhere. The other room was sparsely furnished with two sofas and a couple of small tables. But one complete wall was shelved from floor to ceiling and laden with books of every description.

Then she broke all the rules and began to climb the stairs. Her steps made no sound on the carpeted treads and although she knew she shouldn't be doing this, shouldn't be intruding on his privacy, she felt compelled to see where he slept, where he wrote his books, knowing that it would bring her closer to knowing him. At the top she moved stealthily along the landing past two small boxrooms towards an open door at the far end. She could make out a large desk covered in paper and books with an angled lamp attached to the side.

She poked her head around the door and received the shock of her life. Rhett Drayton lay asleep in an old-fashioned brass bed at the other end of the room! His breathing was steady. Sarah bit back an audible gasp. She remembered the conversation at dinner that first night when Isobel had mentioned Rhett's all-night writing shifts and she could have kicked herself for not realising that just because he hadn't answered her calls downstairs, it didn't mean he wasn't in.

She panicked, thinking that he might wake suddenly and find her in his room staring at him and she tiptoed quickly and quietly down the stairs before anything so harrowing could occur.

Back in the scullery she relaxed again, but all sense of propriety left her then and on impulse she decided to clean up the scullery for him before she left.

She closed the door between the scullery and the hallway in case any noise disturbed him and put the kettle on while she set about putting the place to rights. She was almost done when the scullery door burst open and a sleepy-eyed Rhett Drayton appeared in the doorway wrapped in a dark green towelling dressing-gown but also wearing a face like thunder. It was obvious he was not pleased to see her at all.

'What on earth do you think you're doing?' he yelled, making her jump and drop one of the mugs she was drying.

It smashed to pieces on the stone floor and Sarah remained rooted to the spot, suddenly aware that this had not been one of her brightest ideas.

'I brought a basket over from Beth and I thought no one was in,' she lied. 'I was just helping, doing a bit of cleaning up, having a break from cleaning paintings. That's all.'

'Well, I was in,' Rhett grumbled, 'and all your incessant clattering has woken me up.'

'Look, I'm really sorry,' Sarah grovelled. 'I can see now what a stupid idea it was, but I really was only trying to help.'

'Were you?' he said. 'Are you sure that's all you were doing? I mean, why on earth would you want to clean up my mess unless you had an ulterior motive?'

'What do you mean?'

'What do you want from me?'

'Nothing,' Sarah managed to stammer.

'Then why not just leave me alone and get on with the job you came here for? It's the house, isn't it? That's what you're after.'

Sarah was upset.

'After the house?' she repeated, puzzled. 'What do you mean?'

Rhett looked exasperated.

'The restoration project you're hankering after, a country house to restore, a reason to leave London. I'm not daft. I must appear rich to you and I've got what you want. Is that it? You think I'm your one-way ticket to a life of luxury and as much restoration as you want. What are you? A new breed of yuppy gold-digger?'

His words were stinging and unfair.

'No. It's not like that at all,' Sarah threw back at him.

'Oh, I think it is,' he carried on. 'I happen to like living this way, on my own. So, if you don't mind, I'd like you to go, now.'

He stood leaning against the scullery door staring at Sarah. With his hair all ruffled and his chin in need of a shave he looked decidedly rough and Sarah felt tears welling up in her eyes. She wasted no more time trying to explain and defend herself, but turned and fled out of the house like a frightened rabbit, his cruel words echoing inside her head. And she'd left the empty basket behind!

Once outside, she ran blindly through the trees until the gatehouse was well out of sight and found that she was running in the direction of the beach. She kept on going until she came to the cliff edge. Crude, rocky steps had been cut into it and over the years had worn down and now made a fairly easy passage down to the seashore.

She took in great gulps of sea air as she made her way down to the sand and went over and over in her mind what he had said. Was that how she had appeared to him — a gold-digger? Her heart was still pounding and when she reached the first flat rock, she sat down on it and cried for all she was worth. Her and her stupid daydreams. What a fool she had made of herself.

Lady Isobel had made her feel so at home here at Fontingray and it had gone to her head. Fancy thinking Rhett would automatically feel the same way about her. Now she had ruined everything. When the pictures were cleaned and the auction imminent, she would say her goodbyes and return to London. She would try to carry on as before, but it wouldn't ever be the same again. How could it be? How would she be able to forget Rhett Drayton? Her feelings were too strong.

She really hoped he hadn't meant all those awful things he had said to her. Maybe he was just angry and had said the first thing that came into his head.

'Are you OK?' a voice asked.

Sarah stopped blowing her nose and wiping the tears from her eyes as she looked up into the face of Coleen Brooks, Harry's nanny. Sarah looked around her and saw the small boy putting stones into his red bucket just a few yards away.

'Oh, I'm all right. It's nothing, really. I'll be fine in a minute.'

'You don't look it. You look like something has really upset you.'

'I'm just being silly,' Sarah insisted.

Coleen raised her eyebrows.

'You must be the one down from London.'

Sarah managed a smile.

'Yes, that's right,' she said standing up. 'Sarah Harper. I'm doing some cleaning and repairs on some valuable paintings that were discovered in the attic recently. The Draytons are auctioning them next month. They should cause quite a stir in the art world. No one knew they were in existence.'

She was aware she was gabbling.

'Interesting,' Coleen said. 'I'm Coleen Brooks, young Harry's nanny.'

She was a strange-looking girl, tall, willowy, wearing a long green, canvas-looking dress, with no coat and bare feet. The wind blew her red hair out behind her and gave her the appearance of a sea nymph.

She took a packet of cigarettes out of her pocket and offered one to Sarah.

'No thank you, I don't smoke.'

'Neither do I supposedly,' Coleen said with a smirk. 'Don't let on you've seen me with one. It's not good around

Harry. That's why we go for lots of long walks together outside. So I can get my fix. Harry can't split on me yet.'

'What will you do when he starts talking properly?'

Coleen thought for a moment.

'I don't intend to be around that long,' she stated, 'but you didn't hear that either.'

Sarah's tears had dried up and she pushed Rhett and his unkind remarks to the back of her mind.

'You're going to leave?' Sarah asked.

Coleen puffed away on her cigarette and watched Harry digging about in the gritty sand with his little plastic spade.

'It's too quiet here for me. I need a bit more excitement. I'm saving hard and then I intend to go abroad. See the world, you know.'

'That will be hard for Harry,' Sarah commented. 'You've been here all his short life.'

Coleen shrugged her shoulders.

'They'll find a replacement easily

enough. Mr Rhett-I-don't-give-a-dam-Drayton won't lose any sleep over it.'

'You sound as though you don't like him very much,' Sarah said.

'No, I don't. Have you met him?'

Sarah blushed.

'Yes, I have. I think he's rather attractive.'

Coleen inhaled the last of her cigarette and stubbed it out on a rock.

'Looks can be deceiving. Don't tell me you've fallen for him already.'

Coleen gave a little laugh, seeing Sarah's red cheeks.

'Is that why you were crying earlier? Has he said something to upset you?'

Sarah didn't want to reveal anything more to this strange girl who was making her feel slightly uneasy.

'It was nothing, really. I hardly know the man,' Sarah said lightly. 'It was just a misunderstanding.'

'If you'll take my advice,' Coleen said as she leaned forward conspiratorially, 'you'll keep clear of that one.'

'Why's that?' Sarah asked, unsure if

she was going to like whatever it was that Coleen was going to tell her.

'I was rather taken to him, too, not long after I got here. But one afternoon, when Harry was with his grandmother, I came down here on the beach and he . . . well, he made certain advances towards me. Just a kiss and a cuddle really. Well, you know, let's just say that I succumbed to his charms. Afterwards, he sauntered off back to his ivory tower without another word and when I went over to the gatehouse to see him, he was really nasty. Told me not to bother him any more. I was there to look after Harry, nothing else, and what happened between us was a mistake and wouldn't happen again. I mean, he used me and then just threw me aside. I didn't know what to do but I didn't want to lose my job so I said nothing and carried on as though nothing had happened.'

Sarah was horrified.

'He just doesn't seem to me to be the type of person who would behave like that.'

Then she thought about his anger with her earlier and realised that he just could be. Coleen raised her eyebrows.

'He's a wolf in sheep's clothing,' she quoted. 'Don't be fooled. I'm going back now. It's time for Harry's nap. Enjoy your stay.'

'See you again,' Sarah said and waved to them both as Coleen picked up her charge and carried him back up the cliffs.

Sarah was glad to be left alone. Her thoughts were in a turmoil and she felt very lost and far away from reality. She told herself that Rhett Drayton had been right about one thing. She did want his house, but she wanted him, too, and not just as a means to get what she wanted, but because she felt drawn to him. He would never believe her if she told him that she had fallen for him far away from here in the depths of a London bookshop, before she knew who he was, or that he lived in a country house needing restoring.

It sounded so corny she could hardly

believe it herself, and as she sat there wondering where all this was going to end, she began to dismantle the castles she'd built in the air and watched her dreams begin to fade away.

7

'I've been trying to phone you, Sarah,' Amanda scolded. 'Your phone has been switched off. I'm dying to know what happened at the dinner on Saturday.'

'Don't get too excited,' Sarah said despondently.

'Oh. I take it things didn't go too well.'

'You could put it like that,' Sarah said, briefly outlining the direction the evening had taken and gave her friend the details of her disastrous visit to the gatehouse and the escape run to the beach.

'So you see,' Sarah explained, 'he doesn't know I fell for him in London and now he thinks I'm only after the house for my restoration dreams. I've really messed things up.'

'You've got to explain everything to him then,' Amanda told her. 'You can't just leave the situation like this, not if you really do like him.'

Sarah sighed.

'I'm going into Castleford later on, to visit the museum. I need some time away. I'll think about my next move over the skeletons of Aramantha and her sailor. You know, I told you the story about them.'

'Yes, you did,' Amanda replied, 'but they're dead and I'd rather know how this present-day love story is going to end.'

'I'm working on it,' Sarah told her friend, 'but I think I've got a lot of bridges to rebuild. Besides which, if Coleen Brooks's story is true, he may be a first-class rat anyway.'

'I'm sure you don't believe he is,' Amanda pointed out. 'My, you've certainly livened up your life, haven't you? How's the actual job going? Have you found time in between swooning to do any work?'

'It's fine,' Sarah said, without any elaboration. 'You can tell Martin that. I don't want to speak to him at the moment though, so if he asks, say the lines aren't good down here. And please don't tell him any of this.'

'As if I would,' Amanda replied. 'I'll have to go. I've got another call coming in. Speak to you later.'

The line went dead.

Later in the day, Sarah was sitting in a quaint old café in Castleford as the old clock on top of the museum chimed out two o'clock. She ordered coffee and scones. She was in no hurry to get back to Fontingray that afternoon and was enjoying her little excursion into the quiet town. She'd spent several hours touring round the museum and had seen the skeletons, reputedly Aramantha and her sailor lover. Sarah had found it all the more interesting having already toured the house with Isobel.

Sarah was watching the passing groups of people, enjoying her delicious scone and cream when her attention was suddenly taken by the sight of a tall, red-haired young woman with a young child. It was Coleen Brooks, exiting from the door of the pub opposite, which held a sign, Children's Room. She was wearing another long dress, this time rust-coloured, topped with a lacy beige cardigan. Following her was a scruffy-looking individual with short black spiky hair and torn jeans. Sarah didn't like the look of him at all, and he was having some sort of argument with Coleen.

The man kept shaking his head violently then looking up to the sky in exasperation. He pushed at Coleen and she suddenly slapped him on the face. Sarah's interest was glued. The man grabbed her arm and held on to her while he shouted something at her. She was hanging on to Harry and putting one hand up to her forehead as though she had a headache. The man rubbed her arm and put his arm round her comfortingly. Sarah couldn't begin to guess what might be going on.

She watched closely as Coleen spoke intently to the man and he started nodding as though he was better pleased. They walked over to a green car parked in the carpark and Coleen opened the back door and began to strap Harry into his safety seat. Safely harnessed, Coleen turned again to her companion and they surprised Sarah by embracing each other and kissing rather passionately before Coleen got into the car and drove off in the direction of Fontingray. Her friend got into a rusty blue jalopy with a red wing and drove off in the opposite direction.

Sarah stared after him until he was out of sight and wondered what on earth that meeting had been about. She certainly didn't like the look of him and wondered if perhaps he had been threatening Coleen. Perhaps she had got herself into some kind of trouble and that was her reason for wanting to leave Harry and her job and disappear off round the world.

Even though Sarah had met the girl only the once she felt concerned and wondered what to do. After she had paid her bill, she went outside and crossed the road to the pub and entered it via the door to the children's room. It was stark and characterless with a small bar at one end. There was no one there but Sarah could see through to the main bar where it appeared to be bustling with customers.

It was a few moments before one of the bar staff saw Sarah and came to serve her, obviously wondering why she was standing alone in the children's room with not a child in sight.

'Yes, please?' he asked.

'An orange and a packet of crisps,' she ordered, not sure why she was there or indeed what she was going to say.

While the young man was filling her glass, Sarah gathered her thoughts and asked him, 'Did you serve that couple that were just in here with the little dark-haired boy. The woman with the red hair?'

'Yes, I did. Why do you want to know that?'

'Well,' Sarah said, 'I was across the

street when they left and I'm sure that I know them from somewhere. I just can't place them for the moment. You don't happen to know their names, do you?'

'I don't know her,' he said, 'but she's been in quite a lot lately with him. His name is Peter Bates. He's a local lad, and he's always in trouble with the law. A bit of a thug, you know, into drugs and petty theft. I'd give him a wide berth if I were you.'

On the way back to Fontingray Sarah wondered what had made her enquire in the pub about Coleen and her friend. It had been a spur-of-the-moment thing, but after watching their disagreement in the carpark Sarah had a funny feeling about him.

When she got back to the manor and went to park her car she noticed one of the other garages was open and she could see Rhett's red car inside. Outside the garage, there was a pool of water over the courtyard and soap suds draining away. For a moment, Sarah thought Rhett had been cleaning his car, until she saw old Sam pottering about. She realised that Rhett wouldn't clean his car while he had staff who could do it.

She waved at Sam and walked off in the direction of the sea instead of the house. She might bump into Coleen again. She knew that really she should get back to the house, do a couple more hours' work, but a while longer wouldn't hurt. She climbed down the familiar stone steps in the side of the cliff and made her way down to the sea shore. The tide was already a good way out, exposing lumps of dark, limpet-laden rocks, seaweed and rock pools.

The beach was deserted, there was no sign of Coleen at all. Sarah took off her boots and socks and wandered along the sand, liking the feel of it between her toes. She was still restless, and if she had thought that these few weeks away from London were just what she needed, now she had her doubts. She was feeling more unsettled than ever and she supposed she had Rhett Drayton to thank for that.

As though the mere thought of the man had conjured him up, Sarah looked ahead of her and saw him approaching her from the other end of the cove. To turn and walk away now would be obvious and cowardly so she carried on walking towards him even though her instincts said to retreat gracefully. He had seen her anyway and seemed to be making a beeline for her. She wondered what he would have to say for himself.

She'd only ever seen him in black jeans or black trousers, but today he was wearing faded blue jeans, tan boots and a blue denim jacket. Somehow that made him seem less intimidating. He stopped a few feet from her and for a moment he just stared. Sarah wouldn't speak first and make it easy for him. She stared back and waited expectantly.

'Hi,' he said feebly.

Sarah greeted him with the same

monosyllable and waited for him to elaborate.

'Look,' he began, staring down at his boots for inspiration, and Sarah was glad to see he looked remorseful, 'about yesterday.'

Sarah gave him a non-committal look.

'I want to apologise,' he said, and he did look as though he meant it. 'I shouldn't have spoken to you like that, said the things I said. It was totally uncalled for and it wasn't what I meant to say at all. It all came out wrong.'

'Did it?' Sarah asked. 'It sounded perfectly clear to me, but maybe I deserved some of it.'

Rhett stuck his hands into his pockets and moved around some sand with his booted foot as Sarah continued.

'I shouldn't have intruded into your house like I did. I'm sorry, too. I really was only trying to help,' she added. 'I'm just a tidy person. I don't like mess and dirty dishes.'

'I do clean up once a week,' he said.

Sarah raised her hands.

'You do just whatever you want. Don't mind me. It is your place.'

While they stood there talking for a few minutes, large clouds rolled in from the sea as quickly as the waves themselves and big spots of rain fell on to Sarah's face and hair. Rhett looked up.

'That's sudden,' he said, and as the heavens opened without a warning he grabbed Sarah's hand. 'Quickly, this way,' he said, dragging her up the beach towards the foot of the craggy cliffs and to an old hut.

Sarah saw where they were going and ran faster, trying to get in before she got too drenched.

'Phew,' she puffed, as they ran inside and shut the door quickly.

She shook the rain from her hair and wiped the droplets from her face.

'Where did that come from so suddenly?' she gasped and looked about her as Rhett shut the door.

They were standing in a seldom-used fisherman's hut.

'It won't last long,' Rhett assured her. 'This will shelter us for a bit. Some of the estate workers use it now and then. It's quite cosy.'

Sarah disagreed. It smelled heavily of fish and seaweed, but at least it would keep them dry until the squall passed. There were several lobster pots dotted about which had been made into makeshift seating with piles of old sacking. Sarah sat down and plonked her boots on the floor, stuffing her socks inside. Rhett sat next to her, pushing his long legs out in front of him and making himself comfortable.

'Pity there's no tea-making facilities,' he commented.

Sarah sat silently, tea far from her thoughts at that moment.

'Am I forgiven?' he asked.

'Well, you saved me from getting completely drenched, so I suppose the answer is yes,' Sarah conceded, 'although it wasn't entirely your fault.'

'What do you mean?'

Sarah debated whether to come clean and bare her soul to him.

'You remember that day in London when you went into the parking space I'd seen?'

Rhett nodded.

'Well, I saw you again in Samson's bookshop and, well, to tell the truth, I spied on you between the shelves and found you . . . well . . . you know . . . I found you very attractive and I couldn't stop thinking about you. There! I've said it. Now you know that I fell for you in London before I even knew you had a country house that was falling down and needed restoring,' and she went on to explain how she had had no intention of trying to get at his house, however it had appeared.

Rhett laughed and had the decency to look flattered.

'I can see how surprised you must have been to come all the way down here and bump into me again.'

'Surprised is an understatement,'

Sarah said, relaxing a little with him, 'but that's not all. I saw you again when you came to Holberns to arrange for my visit and then again in Sardi's restaurant.'

'Really?' he said. 'What a coincidence. I hardly ever go to London.'

Sarah took the bull by the horns.

'Who was the woman you had dinner with?'

Rhett paused, recognising Sarah's jealousy.

'My agent, Tamsin Weekes. I'd just done a book signing that day and we were celebrating record first-day sales.'

Sarah was relieved.

'Congratulations,' she managed to blurt out.

'She's married, too,' Rhett said, smiling at her.

Sarah was acutely aware that now she'd laid all her cards on the table and Rhett knew exactly how she felt about him, but she was still completely in the dark about whether he liked her or not.

She felt like a silly, love-sick schoolgirl with a crush on a teacher.

'The thing is,' Sarah continued, 'after all those encounters with you, I kept thinking about you and by the time I arrived at Fontingray and saw you again, you were indelibly imprinted on my mind and in my thoughts constantly, so it was as though I knew you already. But, of course, we'd barely spoken and you had no idea who I was.'

Rhett looked uncomfortable.

'Look,' he said, 'don't think that I don't find you attractive. You are, very. It's just . . . '

Sarah jumped up. She didn't want to hear what he was going to say, something corny like it was too soon after his wife had died, that he wasn't ready for any kind of friendship, or that he could never make her happy. She just didn't want to hear any of it, especially here in the confines of an old fishing hut with the rain pounding on the corrugated tin roof and the wind whipping the waves into a white frenzy.

'Please, you don't have to explain. Really, there's no need.'

She stared out of the grimy, little window, out to sea, wishing herself miles away from here. She could just make out a small vessel bobbing about on the ocean. Oh, to be transported on to that boat.

She heard him get up behind her and her heart was battering her chest so heavily she could hear it pounding in her ears and thumping in her throat. She dared not turn around and face him but she was aware that he was standing but a hair's breadth from her. She almost held her breath as he pulled her round to face him.

'I am guilty of flirting with you, when I first saw you in the library at the house, but when you said that you wanted to get away from London, all that stuff about a restoration project, well, you can't blame me for getting the wrong impression. I'm sorry, really. I've got another confession to make, too. I've been watching you while you work.'

Sarah gasped.

'What?' she asked, the words barely audible.

'From the minstrels' gallery,' he admitted.

Sarah was furious.

'How dare you spy on me!' she said angrily, trying to shrug free from where he had his hand on her shoulder.

She made for the door, struggling with the latch, but he went round her and put his weight against it preventing her from opening it, blocking her escape.

'You trespassed in my house,' he accused her.

'That's not the same,' she said, trying to dismiss the fact that she had also crept up into his room and watched him sleeping!

She tried to push him aside.

'Let me out, please,' she said, feeling dizzy from the sheer closeness of him and the touch of his hands on her.

'I don't think you mean that,' he said and, impulsively, he pulled her into his arms bringing his lips down hard on hers.

It was impossible for her to struggle. This was something she had yearned for, ever since she had set eyes on him and now she melted against him and returned his kiss urgently. Then he backed off and leaned against the door, closing his eyes.

'I'm sorry,' he said. 'I shouldn't have done that.'

'No, no, it's OK,' Sarah said. 'Really, I . . . '

'No, you don't understand,' he said. 'I'm sorry. I'd better just go.'

All sorts of emotions were coursing through her body. The rain had stopped. Rhett opened the hut door. He turned, looking back at her as he stepped outside, and he went to say something, but changed his mind. He walked quickly away from her and left her standing alone in the hut, staring after his receding figure. She wondered if it had been a dream and she was going to wake up in a minute, but she could still taste him on her lips.

She sat down on the lobster pots and began pulling on her socks and boots while trying to make sense of everything, but she couldn't work it out. He was a mystery.

She waited at least half an hour before setting off back to the house to make sure she gave Rhett enough time to disappear, if that's what he wanted. On the way back through the wood, with the leaves dripping over her, she kept hearing Coleen's words to her the day before.

'He just used me and then threw me aside.'

What was the matter with him, Sarah thought.

She knew there had been a spark of chemistry between them that first day in the library. He as much as admitted that he found her attractive. Not only that, he'd been spying on her whilst she had been working and now the kiss. So why the big drama? It didn't make sense. Was he still so upset about the death of his wife? Was that the reason he was resisting them getting to know each other better?

8

She turned it over and over in her mind as she approached the house through the now familiar grounds. It was four-thirty and she wondered if she had been missed, if anything would be said about her leaving her work for most of the day and taking time off. Then, as she rounded the corner of the main house, a police car and ambulance came into view.

The first thing that crossed her mind was that maybe one of the estate workers had had an accident but she dismissed that because the vehicles were parked outside the main entrance. Her heart missed a beat, and she gave an involuntary shiver as she made her way quickly down the steps to the side door and hurried along to the kitchen. It was deserted and eerily quiet for that time of day when dinner was usually being prepared.

She went through the door at the far end and along the passage to the stairs that led up into one of the many hallways. Silence greeted her. What had happened? She went along to the Old Hall and stared at the painting she was working on. It was a scene from a London street during the time of the plague. Quaint, little Tudor buildings had their doors daubed with red crosses and people were bringing their dead out into the street. It was disturbing and shocking.

She threw on the lights surrounding it and picked up her tools to catch up on some work. She would find out soon enough who had needed the emergency services. She rubbed away expertly at the bottom corner of the painting, gently at first, but when Rhett's face appeared in her mind again, she started scrubbing vigorously with pent-up frustration.

When she realised what she was doing, it was too late. The centuries-old paint she had been cleaning had actually dissolved beneath her fingers and gone for ever!

'Oh, no!' she cried out loud, and quickly looked around as though she expected an audience watching her mistake.

How on earth was she going to explain that? She'd never misjudged her technique like that before. She slammed down the gauze cloth on the floor. Mr Rhett Drayton was the cause of this! But how could she explain that to Sir Hugh and Lady Isobel, or Martin!

She sat down on the nearest chair and took comfort in the tears that rolled quietly down her cheeks. Gradually, through her distress, she heard a knock, quiet at first, then louder and the door opened. A red-eyed Beth pushed the door wider and stood back to admit the police officers.

Sarah jumped up, at once alarmed. They strolled purposefully towards her, their shoes squeaking as they walked. The policeman, thick-set and rather intimidating, looked straight at her, gauging her reaction to their arrival. The other officer, a woman, looked around the hall and took in the surroundings.

'Sarah Harper?' the policeman asked.

'Yes,' she replied. 'What's happened?'

'I'm Detective-Sergeant Rawlings,' he continued, 'and this is Woman Police Officer Davies. There was an incident here earlier this afternoon. You may be able to help us with our enquiries.'

Sarah was completely puzzled, and couldn't think what she could possibly know that would help them solve a crime. She began to feel worried and the policewoman stepped forward. She had a soft, calming voice.

'Do you know Coleen Brooks, the Draytons' nanny?' she asked.

Sarah was careful with her answer as though she were under suspicion for something.

'I don't know her well,' she answered. 'I've only met her once since I've been staying here. We bumped into each other on the beach yesterday, while she was out with Harry. We talked for a few minutes, that's all.'

'What did you talk about?' Rawlings asked.

Sarah thought about the question quickly. She didn't want to tell them that Coleen had told her she wanted to leave the job and go off round the world, or that she disliked Rhett Drayton. She didn't know what had happened or how Coleen might be involved.

'Not much really,' she said. 'We just introduced ourselves, talked about the weather and what I was doing here.'

Rawlings looked at the painting on the easel.

'Yes, you're down from London, aren't you, cleaning pictures for an auction?'

Sarah nodded and he continued.

'Did you know any of the Draytons before you came down here to work for them?'

'No,' she began. 'Well, yes, sort of.'

Rawlings raised his eyebrows at her. 'Yes or no?'

Sarah was feeling decidedly uncomfortable and even guilty — of what though? She found herself telling the two officers how she had bumped into Rhett Drayton on several occasions before her visit, but that she had no idea who he was, until she arrived.

'You are a long way from home,' Rawlings observed. 'Is it a regular thing, working away from London, in country houses?'

'No, it's usually all done in-house,' Sarah told him. 'Sir Hugh didn't want to send us the paintings, however. He wanted someone to come down. I was selected.'

Rawlings pondered this for a moment, taking in the information, lining up his next question. Sarah's hands were clammy and she was shaking a bit. She'd never been questioned by the police before and she felt foolish for reacting in such a negative way. Did they notice that? She expected so. They were trained in interrogation, weren't they?

'What made you accept this assignment, then?' Rawlings continued.

'I was fed-up with London,' Sarah told him, 'and it was a welcome change. I love country houses and I'm really enjoying being here. Look, where is this all leading? What has happened?'

WPC Davies took a turn in the proceedings.

'Sometime this afternoon between two o'clock and four o'clock, Harry Drayton was kidnapped. Coleen Brooks was knocked unconscious during the attack.'

'Oh, good heavens!' Sarah exclaimed. 'I can't believe it. Oh, no!'

She thought immediately about Rhett. How had he reacted? But she kept her thoughts to herself. She was an outsider after all.

'Where were you this afternoon between those times?' Rawlings asked.

Sarah's mind suddenly went into overdrive. She had seen Coleen and

Harry in Castleford just after two o'clock with that awful man. If he was Coleen's boyfriend and she didn't want her employers to know about him, then Sarah didn't want to cause a fuss by bringing him to everyone's attention.

'I went into Castleford at about noon and visited the museum,' she answered. 'Then I went and had some tea in the Copper Pot. After that I came back here.'

'What time did you get back?'

'I'm not sure exactly. About three o'clock, I think.'

'Did you come straight back to the house?'

'No,' Sarah admitted. 'I went down to the beach for a walk first.'

She thought about her meeting with Rhett on the beach. This questioning was very difficult when you didn't want to give everything away.

'Did you see anyone? Notice anything suspicious?'

She had to mention Rhett in case they had questioned him and he had mentioned seeing her. What if he hadn't though? Blast him again, she thought.

'I did see Mr Rhett Drayton, out walking,' she said. 'We spoke a few words, that was all. There was no one else around.'

'Didn't you get caught in that rainstorm?' WPC Davies asked.

Sarah gave a little laugh.

'Nearly. There was an old fishing hut at the foot of the cliffs. I dashed in there until it stopped. Then I wandered back here and started work again at about half-past four.'

'We think the incident took place between two and four, but we'll be able to verify that when Miss Brooks regains consciousness.'

'What's going to happen now?' Sarah asked anxiously.

'I've got a team coming down to tap into the phone line in case a ransom is demanded. WPC Davies will stay here with the Draytons, I shall go to the hospital and wait for Miss Brooks to come round, see if she can shed more light on the attack. I don't think she's too badly injured.'

'Thank goodness for that,' Sarah said. 'I just hope that little boy is OK. It must be awful for the family.'

WPC Davies saw her concerned look.

'If it is a kidnap for ransom he's bound to be kept well. They'll want to guarantee their money.'

'What if it's not?' Sarah asked.

'It's better not to think about that unless we have to,' she answered, and Sarah gave a shudder.

'Right,' Rawlings said, 'that's all for now. I'll probably be back again. In the meantime if you can think of anything that you've seen this past week, anything odd, anyone taking an interest in the estate and its layout, well, let me or WPC Davies know.'

'I will certainly give it some thought,' Sarah said as they turned to go.

Early that evening, Sarah was seated at the little pine table in the kitchen watching Beth loading the dumb-waiter with the Draytons' evening meal.

'I still can't believe it,' Beth was saying. 'Right under our noses. You just wouldn't credit it, would you?'

'It's awful,' Sarah agreed, as Lucy dished up some dinner for herself, Sarah and Beth.

Lucy usually ate with them before going home for the day. She placed the meal in front of Sarah, and sat down to hers opposite.

'How you managed to produce a meal this evening with all that going on I don't know,' Sarah admired. 'You must be worried sick.'

'You just have to carry on,' Beth replied. 'Whether they'll eat this or not is another matter. Lady Isobel was crying when I left her and Sir Hugh and Rhett are just arguing about the security of the estate.'

'I wonder how Harry is?' Lucy said quietly.

'I expect he's missing Coleen,' Sarah said. 'She's like a mum to him.'

That set Beth off again.

'I'll just serve this up for them,' she sobbed, as she hoisted the ropes on the dumb-waiter and the trays shot upwards.

'I'm sure Harry will be OK,' Sarah said optimistically. 'Let's hope Coleen is, too, and is back home again quickly. I wonder if she has come round.'

Lucy still seemed to have her appetite in spite of all the goings on.

'Have you met Coleen?' she asked Sarah after Beth had gone.

'Only once, on the beach yesterday,' she replied. 'Why?'

'What did you think of her?'

Sarah thought for a moment.

'A bit strange, but all right, I suppose,' she said. 'Don't you like her?'

'I don't think she should be a nanny.'

'What makes you say that?' Sarah asked, puzzled. 'I thought she was good with Harry.'

'She wasn't today, was she?'

'Well, that wasn't exactly Coleen's fault. I'm sure she didn't want him kidnapped. Look what happened to her, hit on the head.'

Lucy shrugged her shoulders.

'She's a bit of a tart.'

Sarah poured some more gravy over her meal and looked up at Lucy.

'Is that just your assumption or do you know she is?' she said bluntly.

'My sister was in her class at school. She was always chasing the boys.'

'That's not abnormal for a schoolgirl, is it?' Sarah said.

'Not just that,' Lucy continued, 'before I started working here I saw something.'

'Oh, what was that?'

Lucy had Sarah's undivided attention.

'About two years ago, I used to come through the estate and sneak down to the beach to sunbathe. It was really secluded. No one else used to go there.'

Sarah could see this was leading somewhere, and was listening very attentively.

'I was tucked away behind a rock, minding my own business, when I saw

Rhett Drayton walking along the beach. He often does, but I was well hidden so he didn't notice me. Coleen had only been here a few months then I think and it must have been her afternoon off, because she was walking along the beach towards him, on her own. They met up just beyond the rock where I was sunbathing so I kept really quiet. They were there for ages, talking. Coleen had a real crush on him, I could tell. She was flirting like mad and I could hear every word. It was embarrassing, and so obvious. Anyway, Rhett was trying to ignore all her advances. I mean, he'd only just buried his wife a few months earlier. I could tell he didn't want anything to do with her. She kept asking if she could bring baby Harry round to the gatehouse to see him and all that. I was peeking round the rock. I saw him start to walk away and guess what?'

'What?' Sarah said.

'Coleen threw her arms around his neck and I heard her say she could give him all the comfort he needed and, well, you know, all that.'

'What did he do?' Sarah asked.

'Well, he pushed her away from him and she fell on to the sand. Then he told her to get lost and stop bothering him, that she was there to look after his son and nothing else. Then he marched off and left her shouting at him. She was shouting that he'd be sorry, and calling him all kinds of horrible names.'

'Gosh,' Sarah said. 'She seemed OK when I spoke to her, quiet and gentle.'

She remembered Coleen's version of these same events and couldn't see any advantage in Lucy fabricating a story like that. More likely Coleen had invented it to save face.

'Did you tell any of this to the police when they questioned you?'

Lucy was shaking her head as Beth returned, still dabbing her eyes. She looked at the kitchen clock.

'You get off home now, my love,' she said to Lucy. 'Your mum will be wondering where you are. She'll think

I'm a slave driver.'

'What about the dishes?' Lucy asked.

'I'll help Beth with them tonight,' Sarah suggested. 'It'll take my mind off things.'

So Sarah and Beth ended the day together in the kitchen, pondering over Coleen, wondering about Harry.

'Mr Rhett seems really upset,' Beth said sadly. 'I do feel sorry for him. I know he hasn't exactly been a model father to the little one, but he does love him. It's just that he's had a really hard time. It must be a constant reminder to him of his wife.'

'What was she like?' Sarah asked.

'Very nice,' Beth recalled. 'Quiet and efficient. She always had a friendly word for the staff, you know, and didn't put on any airs and graces. You remind me of her in some ways.' Beth surprised Sarah. 'You've got similar mannerisms and something about the eyes. It's uncanny.'

She wiped her hands on her apron and started putting the dishes away in the cupboard, thanking Sarah for her help.

As Sarah made her way wearily to her room, armed with another couple of books from Fontingray's inexhaustible supply, she thought about Beth's remarks and considered whether her resemblance to Bridie had been noticed by Rhett, too. Maybe that was why he was keeping her at arm's length. She also had in her thoughts the disaster that had occurred with the painting. Her head was in a turmoil about how she was going to rectify the problem. It was a long while before she fell asleep that night and her dreams were filled with kidnappers, art thieves and forgers.

9

Sarah woke in a very black mood the next day. She'd had a restless night, and when she remembered the events of the previous day and the accident she'd had with the painting her mood turned even blacker. She was anxious to get down to the hall to examine what she'd done.

She inspected the painting with a stronger magnifying glass and wasn't sure at first if she believed what she was seeing. Even though she had only read about pictures being painted on top of others she instinctively knew that she had accidentally found something important. She turned the painting round to look at the back. Why hadn't she noticed it before? The original painting she had been cleaning had been dated in the eighteenth century, but the frame and the type of canvas used showed it to be much older than that.

There was also something written on the back, in French, which seemed out of place on a painting of a London scene by an English painter. She was certain she was on to something all right, and started cleaning and scraping away more of the top layer. It seemed to be coming off easier than she thought it would and her heart started beating faster as she exposed a definite image underneath and part of a signature.

When she went to have her lunch in the kitchen with Beth and Lucy, she was dying to tell them what she had discovered but their mood was sombre and Sarah knew it wasn't the right time. Beth relayed the events of the morning.

'Coleen arrived back at about eleven o'clock. That big policeman brought her back.'

'How is she?' Sarah asked.

'She's got a huge bash on her head. Poor girl. She's really upset.'

'She was crying when I went up,' Lucy added.

'Is anyone with her?' Sarah said.

'That policewoman was earlier, but I think she left her to go to sleep. I've made Coleen a sandwich. I don't know if she'll want it.'

Sarah offered to take it up with a pot of tea.

'Just to let her know we're all thinking of her,' she said.

Beth thought it was a nice gesture and handed Sarah a tray, with a plate of sandwiches and a pot of tea.

Coleen was lying half propped up in bed when Sarah knocked on the door and went in. She hadn't been over to this part of the house when Isobel had shown her around and she realised just how big and rambling the place was. Coleen looked up as Sarah entered the room, her eyes red and swollen.

'Hi,' Sarah greeted the patient, who sported a large dressing on the side of her head and a black eye.

'Hi. I thought you were the police again.'

Sarah put the tray down on an empty table.

'Have they been questioning you?'

'Ever since I came round.' She sighed. 'I wish they'd just leave me alone. I don't know any more than I've told them, but they keep going on and on.'

Sarah commiserated with her.

'They're only doing their job. You want them to find Harry, don't you?'

Coleen started crying again and Sarah took that as a yes.

'I've brought you a sandwich and some tea.'

'I'm not hungry.'

'It will make you feel better.'

Sarah passed her some more tissues from a box on the bedside table and looked around Coleen's room while the girl blew her nose and dried her eyes. It was a pretty room, full of light from three tall windows. Each had a window seat and plumped-up cushions. The walls were papered in soft greens and peaches and it had been made into a bed-sit, with everything Coleen would need, even cooking facilities, for Harry's meals. Two further doors revealed glimpses of Harry's bedroom and a bathroom.

Sarah made herself busy pouring some tea out for Coleen, then drew a seat up next to the bed.

'You don't mind me coming, do you?' she asked. 'I'll go if you don't want me here.'

Coleen turned her head to the wall.

'Stay if you like,' she said.

'I thought you might like to talk to someone other than police officers and the Draytons,' she replied. 'How's the head?'

'Sore,' Coleen replied, then she gave a deep sigh and started to cry again. 'Oh, what a mess this is, and it's all my fault.'

'Of course it isn't,' Sarah scolded. 'You didn't ask to be hit over the head. Did you see who did it?'

Coleen shook her head into the pillow.

'He came up behind me. I'd just put Harry in his cot for his nap. I didn't even hear the door open.'

'It was a man then?' Sarah asked.

Coleen paused.

'Well, I don't know. I didn't see them. I just assumed.'

'It must have happened so quickly you didn't see it coming. You poor thing.'

Tears were streaming down Coleen's face again. She closed her eyes and Sarah thought she was going to go to sleep again.

'Poor little thing,' Coleen spluttered. 'I wish it hadn't happened this week. He's got a cough.'

'I don't think there's ever a good time to get kidnapped,' Sarah observed.

'I hope he looks after him. He forgot to pick up the bottle of cough mixture I got from the chemist.'

Sarah had the feeling she wasn't really welcome and was standing up and putting the chair back.

'I'm going to go now,' she said. 'You look tired. Try and drink some tea and have another sleep. I'm sure things will work out all right. The police know their job.'

Coleen barely acknowledged her leaving. She was muttering to herself into a fist full of soggy tissues. Sarah closed the door gently behind her.

She was feeling weary herself after the restless night she'd had. She decided to go for a little outing to Castleford library to see if any information could be found about the artist whose work she had stumbled on. It was quite exciting to think that she was the first person to set eyes on it for a long time. It was a shame that the excitement of it had been marred by Harry's kidnapping.

She soon discovered several references to the artist. He was a Frenchman by the name of Henry B. le Seuyare and the book said he had died a poor man by all accounts. It wasn't until the nineteenth century that his work had begun to be recognised as the work of a genius and his paintings had been highly sought after, fetching very high prices at auction.

Many of his works had been stolen from a chateau in France just before the First World War and had never been seen again. Six more in a private collection had been destroyed by fire in a country house in the Midlands. The book went on to say that three paintings had been discovered in a house in Sussex in 1913 together with their provenance. Two cropped up at auction sixty years later and fetched eight and a half million pounds each! The third was never found. In today's market it would be worth in excess of eighteen million pounds if it ever came to light.

Sarah was trembling all over by this time and was glad she was seated in a quiet corner of the library where she couldn't be seen. She had a grin on her face that she couldn't get rid of. This was more like the adventure she'd had in mind when she'd arrived at Fontingray! Fancy Beth telling her that nothing ever happened there. She had fallen in love, a little boy had been kidnapped and now it looked as though a priceless work of art had come to light after being concealed in a dusty attic for nearly a century.

If the painting she had discovered was the missing Seuyare, it was probable that it had been painted over the top of by a forger to disguise it so it could be smuggled out of France. The date on it had probably been bogus. Sarah wondered if the provenance had been in the attic, too, and if so, was it still there?

Her head was buzzing so much from all the events of the past few days she had developed a headache. She put the book back on the shelf and went outside for some fresh air. There was an old-fashioned chemist shop just across the road, so she made her way over to it with the intention of buying some headache tablets.

The bell tinkled over the door as she went in. There were several customers and Sarah took her place in the queue. Her attention was drawn to the customer at the head of the queue. A young man in scruffy jeans with black spiky hair was asking for some disposable nappies and a bottle of cough mixture for a child.

Coleen's voice came back to Sarah then saying, 'He forgot to take the cough mixture.'

Just then the man turned around to leave the shop and Sarah recognised the youth Coleen had argued with the day before in the pub carpark. Sarah left the shop right on his heels, all thoughts of her headache gone. She watched him get into the same rusty blue car with the red wing and drive off. She memorised the number plate and jotted it down on the back of an envelope from her handbag.

Surely it wasn't what she was thinking! It couldn't have been him who took Harry. And more to the point, was Coleen in on it? She stood there staring up the road as the car disappeared.

10

As Sarah approached the sitting-room where Lady Isobel, Sir Hugh and Rhett were all waiting together for news, the door opened and WPC Davies came out into the corridor.

'Hello, Miss Harper,' she said, and held the door open for her. 'Are you just going in?'

'No,' Sarah told her. 'Actually, I was looking for you. I may have some information that could be useful.'

The policewoman's expression altered. 'Oh, right,' she said. 'Come and sit over here and talk to me about it.'

She led Sarah towards the end of the corridor where there was a recess containing a gilt-edged sofa. They both sat down and the policewoman asked Sarah what it was that she knew.

'I'm not really sure where to start,' Sarah said. 'I mean, none of it was really significant to start with, not until I went into the chemist. Then it all started to slip into place.'

WPC Davies looked intrigued.

'Take it slowly,' she said, 'just as you remember it. I'll write it all down, then we'll sort it out.'

She opened her notebook and with pen poised, she looked at Sarah and waited patiently for her to gather her thoughts. Sarah began first with her conversation with Coleen on the beach, when Coleen told her of her impending departure and intended world travel. Then she went on to explain Coleen's dislike for Rhett Drayton and how her and Lucy's stories of the same incident weren't the same.

WPC Davies listened intently, scribbling down in her notebook as Sarah started to describe the argument she had witnessed in the pub carpark between Peter Bates and Coleen. Finally, she related Coleen's mumbled words that morning.

'I mean, she said she wished it hadn't

been this week, because of Harry's cough, but surely you would just say, 'I wish it hadn't happened.' It all started to add up then,' Sarah told the policewoman. 'Coleen was quite upset when I saw her this morning. She said it was all her fault.'

'It certainly does sound suspicious,' WPC Davies agreed. 'Taken as a whole, it definitely requires checking. You know, we have actually received a ransom demand in the last hour.'

'Oh, my goodness,' Sarah said.

'It's good you managed to remember the number plate of Mr Bates's car, too. That will help. I have to say, we did have our suspicions that this may be an inside job.'

'Do you think Coleen was involved then?'

'It's quite possible. I'll contact my unit and start the proceedings. I must ask you to keep all this to yourself just for the time being though.'

Sarah nodded.

'Of course, but I feel awful. Suppose

I am wrong about them and they're innocent. Peter Bates may have been buying the medicine for someone else.'

'I would say that was fairly improbable, given all the circumstances,' WPC Davies told her. 'But if they are innocent, you mustn't worry. You only told me what you saw. We have to explore every lead, no matter what. There's a small child at risk here. You mustn't forget that.'

Sarah seemed a bit more relieved and stood up.

'This waiting is dreadful,' she added. 'How is the family coping?'

WPC Davies gave a little shrug.

'They are supporting each other the best they can.'

She indicated her notebook.

'This may just be the lead we were waiting for. The best thing you can do is try and carry on with some of your work. Keep busy. It will help take your mind off the situation for a while, and with a bit of luck we may have some good news before the end of the day.'

'I hope so,' Sarah said. 'Well, if that's all then, I'll do as you suggested and get on with some work.'

The kidnapping had cast a shadow over Sarah's excitement about the painting she had discovered, but at least, before anyone found out what had happened to the painting of the plague scene she had been working on, she would be able to expose some more of the Seuyare underneath and would at least have something substantial to present to the Draytons. She also knew that she was going to have to speak to Martin very soon. He was bound to be wondering why she hadn't been in contact.

At intervals throughout the afternoon, Sarah kept going to the window to see if there was anything happening outside. It was a most frustrating time. She saw Sam trundling around the gardens, tidying up and weeding as though nothing had happened. At around three o'clock, though, she was finally rewarded with the sight of Rhett

Drayton getting into a police car with Rawlings. She watched it move off quickly down the drive.

From the expression on their faces, something was definitely happening at last and Sarah felt the adrenalin begin to pump around her body as she kept her fingers crossed that she had been right and that young Harry had been found. Downing her tools, she left her work and stayed in the library where she could get a better view of the arrivals and departures from the main door.

She was seated at the desk right in front of the window. It commanded a wonderful view of the long drive down to the road and the crescent-shaped turning area around the cherub water-fountain. She was sat there flicking through some back issues of a magazine when two police cars entered the drive. She watched their approach. She burst into tears when she saw Rhett getting out of the first one with Harry, all tousled and wrapped in a blanket. It was a very heart-warming sight and Sarah wished she could be part of it.

Three officers got out of the second car and Sarah stayed glued to the window. Not long after they had entered the house, they left again. This time they had Coleen in tow, still wearing her bandage. As Sarah watched the car disappear with the red-haired girl in the back, flanked by two burly officers, there was a knock at the library door and WPC Davies came in.

'Mrs Drayton said I might find you here,' she said.

Sarah jumped up.

'I've been reading,' she said, 'but I just saw Mr Drayton arrive home with Harry. I'm so glad he's safe. It was Peter Bates then?'

'Yes,' the policewoman said. 'Luckily it was not a very professional attempt at all. Harry's back with his family and none the worse for his ordeal. They are very grateful for the information you gave us. It proved correct and Miss Brooks was involved as well.'

'I saw her going off in the police car,' Sarah told her. 'I can't believe it.'

'The Draytons would like to have a word, if that's all right,' WPC Davies added. 'They're in the sitting-room.'

'Of course,' Sarah said. 'I'll come right away,' and she made her way to the door.

The sitting-room was a much happier place now. Harry was seated on his grandmother's lap eating a biscuit and Beth was bustling about with tea and cakes for everyone. Rawlings was tucking into a huge piece of chocolate cake and a couple of other officers were drinking tea and congratulating everyone on the way things had turned out.

'It's all down to Miss Harper, here,' Rhett said.

Sarah blushed and smiled. She didn't trust herself to speak in case she started crying. The atmosphere was very emotional.

'Don't be so modest,' Rhett said to her, looking at her quite tenderly, in a way Sarah had not experienced before.

'Seriously, though,' he carried on, 'you have been a great help today with your observations. We are all thoroughly grateful. I don't know how to repay you.'

'There's no need, really,' Sarah insisted. 'I'm just so glad that Harry is back safely. I can't begin to imagine what you must have gone through this last twenty-four hours. It must have been a nightmare.'

Rhett lifted Harry up off Isobel's lap and gave him a cuddle.

'I haven't taken much notice of this little chap and he doesn't deserve that. It's not his fault that his mother was taken from us. I realised today how important he was though, when I thought I might not see him again.'

He paused a moment, choking back the tears. He went to speak again but the words wouldn't come out and he buried his face in Harry's hair. Isobel was having a little sob to herself on the sofa, so Sir Hugh took over.

'We are all very grateful to you,

Sarah, very grateful indeed.'

'It's what anyone in my position would have done,' Sarah insisted, feeling rather uncomfortable in the rôle of heroine.

'Well done,' WPC Davies said, 'and now we can leave you all in peace. I'm glad everything turned out as it did.'

Isobel managed to stand up and the police officers started moving towards the door muttering their farewells. Isobel and Hugh followed them, repeating their thanks and good wishes. Harry looked tired out. He was resting his head on his father's shoulder and Sarah smiled at them both. Rhett smiled at her, too. There seemed no need for words.

'Thank goodness that's over,' Isobel said as she came back into the room with Hugh.

She looked over at father and son, liking what she saw.

'I'd better get this chap some tea before he falls asleep,' she said.

Sarah felt as though she was

intruding on this very private family scene.

'Well,' Sir Hugh said, 'I think that's enough excitement for one day. I'm going to the drawing-room to enjoy a nice, fat cigar.'

'Actually,' Sarah began, 'I have something else to tell you all which is rather exciting. I've been dying to say something, but it wasn't the right time.'

All three looked straight at her with similar puzzled looks on their faces, as though none of them could imagine, after the events of the day, what she could possibly tell them that would be any more exciting. She waited a few moments for the suspense to mount then explained to them what had happened to the painting and what she had discovered.

'Oh,' Isobel said, 'I rather liked that plague scene.'

'Be quiet, Isobel,' Sir Hugh said sharply, and looked back to Sarah. 'What exactly are you saying then? That we have a painting sitting downstairs that could fetch millions? Are you serious?'

'Quite serious. I've checked out all the details in a book at Castleford library,' she explained. 'The missing work is of an underwater scene of mermaids and people of an imaginary undersea world, and that seems to be precisely what I am uncovering.'

'Well, I'll be blowed. I'm staggered,' Sir Hugh said, sitting down. 'This is absolutely amazing.'

'And you say,' Rhett continued, 'that a forger painted over the top to hide it? It sounds incredible.'

'Yes,' Sarah told him. 'I know it's hard to believe but I have read about this before. It would make perfect sense if the owners didn't want the painting to be discovered by the enemy as they took it out of France.'

'I can't believe it,' Isobel said, her eyes wide. 'How much is it worth?'

Sarah was anxious not to get them all too excited.

'Quite a lot,' she said cautiously.

'Possibly several millions.'

'We must have a look at this more closely, right away,' Sir Hugh said with great authority.

'There's just one other thing,' Sarah added. 'If you have the provenance that goes with it, that could boost the price even further.'

Isobel was thinking.

'Mermaids?' she said. 'Underwater people?'

Sarah looked at her hopefully.

'In the old attics in the east wing, there is a leather-bound folder which contains some sketches and coloured drawings. I'm sure I recall mermaids and such. There's also some pages written in French.'

'That could just be it,' Sarah said enthusiastically. 'We need to get it down and compare it with the painting.'

Isobel went and took Harry from his father.

'Let me take Harry and see to him then we'll go straight up to the attic and search for the folder.'

Once Harry was tucked up safely in bed, Isobel took charge and led the way up to the old attics in the east wing. As soon as she had described the folder of sketches in detail, they all began pushing around boxes, searching diligently.

'I hope your memory isn't playing games with you,' Sir Hugh said, with a worried look on his face.

But Isobel was adamant that she had seen it, and very soon their frantic search in the subdued light of early evening proved fruitful and they all gazed on the grimy green leather folder in complete awe.

11

The days following Harry's kidnap and the discovery of the Seuyare were very different for Sarah now. The week she had spent quietly working in the Old Hall, with only suits of armour and her daydreams for company, seemed a million miles away.

The calm sea air still hung over the house but the peace and tranquillity had disappeared the moment she had phoned Martin and told him what had happened. He could hardly believe it was true and Isobel and Sarah had gone back to Castleford library to borrow the book Sarah had found so they could study the description of the missing painting and compare it. There was no doubt about it, they had the missing Seuyare.

Then it was all out of Sarah's hands. Martin made arrangements on the phone with Sir Hugh and she no longer felt a part of it. Martin had arrived a day later with a cavalcade which included a firm's van loaded to the hilt with auctioneers equipment and chairs, a security firm to check the security of the premises and lock up the painting, and three colleagues who were experts in French art.

They took over the place and Sarah took refuge in her room on the second evening to escape the hustle and bustle. She phoned Amanda, who was very disappointed to be missing out on all the excitement.

'They've only been here two days,' Sarah moaned, 'and it's bedlam already.'

'Well,' Amanda said, enthusiastically, 'I don't suppose they see a priceless painting every day of the week. Is it really worth millions?'

'That's what they're saying,' Sarah replied. 'I just can't begin to contemplate such an enormous sum of money.'

'You should get a reward,' Amanda

stated. 'It's only fair. After all you made the discovery.'

'I hadn't thought of that,' Sarah replied, 'but I've actually had a rather interesting offer from Lady Isobel that could be very rewarding, under different circumstances.'

Amanda was intrigued.

'What's that then?'

'Well,' Sarah began, 'this afternoon, she said to me that if the painting does fetch what the experts are claiming, then she'll be able to carry out all the restoration and open the house to the public exactly as she planned it.'

'Go on,' Amanda said impatiently.

'Well, she asked me if I would like to be the project manager here.'

'Good grief,' Amanda exclaimed, 'you'll have to leave London.'

'I don't mind that,' Sarah admitted. 'It's lovely down here. I would love to live in Cornwall. I'm just not sure of the job.'

'Not sure of the job?' Amanda

repeated. 'Why ever not? It's just what you want.'

'Not quite,' Sarah corrected her. 'It would mean being around Rhett.'

'I thought you wanted to be around him.'

'I do,' Sarah said, 'but I don't think he wants to be around me.'

'Not even since you explained to him how you felt when you first saw him in London?'

'Nope,' she told Amanda. 'Since then, he's just acted really coolly with me, as though nothing has happened, and since Martin and his team have arrived, Rhett has made himself pretty scarce, and Martin is really getting on my nerves.'

'I wish I could come down there and sort out you lot.' Amanda laughed. 'I'd bang your heads together and knock some sense into them.'

'Thanks for that,' Sarah joked.

'Seriously, though,' Amanda continued, 'accept the job and sort his nibs out later.'

'I'll sleep on it,' Sarah finished, 'and make a decision tomorrow.'

It was three o'clock the next afternoon when Sarah made her decision to go back to London. She was enjoying a brief moment of tranquillity in the Old Hall by herself, and her work on the paintings was almost complete. She would go the next morning. She didn't want to stay for the auction. Martin was visibly suffering in her presence and it was obvious to her that Rhett was avoiding her. So what was the point of prolonging her stay?

She stood in front of the special steel-inforced case that held the Seuyare and gazed at it, daunted by its value, still amazed she had made the discovery. It was ironic that Coleen and her boyfriend had carried out that elaborate plan to kidnap Harry for ransom, which then backfired on them, when all they'd had to do was steal the painting that had been leaning against the wall in the Old Hall for several weeks unattended!

Footsteps approached from behind her. It was Martin.

'It's wonderful, isn't it?' he said, putting an arm around her. 'What a fantastic discovery. A once-in-a-lifetime find.'

Sarah was feeling decidedly uncomfortable around him. He looked around to check that they were alone and before Sarah could see it coming he had produced a jeweller's box and was gazing at her in a strange way.

'You're a once-in-a-lifetime find, too, you know.'

Sarah's mouth dropped open as she suddenly realised what he was doing, and he misread her expression as one of surprise, not sheer panic. He opened the box and the single diamond shone out at her as he spoke.

'We've known each other for some time now and we always get on so well, don't we? I really missed you last week. It made me realise how much you mean to me.'

Sarah tried to speak but no words

came out. She just couldn't stop him.

He was smiling as he asked her, 'Will you marry me?'

Sarah went hot and cold. She wanted to run away but someone had nailed her feet to the floor! So, with a rushing noise in her ears, she closed her eyes and hoped a hole would open in the floor and swallow her up. When she opened them again, she was still standing there, mute, and Martin was waiting for an answer.

She suddenly realised she was shaking her head and a feeling of guilt washed over her as she watched Martin's expression change as he realised that she didn't feel the same way about him.

'The answer's no, isn't it? I can read it in your eyes,' he said and snapped the box shut.

'Oh, Martin,' Sarah managed at last, 'I am so sorry. I had no idea you felt like that. I do like you, I really do, but, as friends only. I can't marry you. I'm really sorry.'

Martin slipped the ring box back into his pocket and turned slowly away from her.

'I feel such a fool,' he said.

Sarah's stomach was in knots and she could feel tears escaping from her eyes and running slowly down her cheeks.

'I feel terrible,' she sobbed and caught hold of his arm but he shrugged it off abruptly.

'Please,' he choked, 'don't!'

Sarah didn't say another word. She just left the room and took herself outside into the sunshine. A warm breeze blew around her, the weather getting ready for a change. Sarah's life was changing, too. It would never be the same again, but she wasn't sure in which direction it was going to go. Her wanderings took her through the rose arbour. Isobel was sitting on one of the benches watching her approach.

'Hello, Sarah. You look deep in thought. Are you still contemplating my job offer?'

Sarah sat on the other end of the

bench and turned to face Isobel.

'I've been thinking hard about it and it's a wonderful opportunity, but I'm just not sure if it's the right thing for me.'

'Why ever not?' Isobel said in surprise. 'I really thought you'd accept without a doubt.'

'I'm just not sure.' Sarah repeated.

'Not sure about what?' Isobel queried. 'Not sure about what Rhett will say?'

Sarah felt herself turn bright scarlet. It was as though Isobel was reading her mind.

'Don't you worry about him,' she continued. 'I think he'll be delighted to see more of you around the place. I've seen the way he looks at you.'

Sarah couldn't cover up her embarrassment, and she couldn't help thinking that Isobel wouldn't have said that if she'd had all the facts or if she'd witnessed their confrontations.

'I'm leaving in the morning to go back to London,' Sarah told her. 'My work on the paintings is complete now.'

Isobel was disappointed.

'You're not going to stay for the auction, after all the excitement of discovering it?'

'I can't,' Sarah told her. 'I have to get back.'

She stood up, not really in the mood to continue this conversation.

'I will pop in and see you before I go.'

'I think you're making a big mistake, Sarah,' Isobel declared, 'and the job offer still stands. Please give it some more thought when you get home. Give me a ring next week if you change your mind.'

Sarah started to walk away.

'OK, I will,' she said.

Isobel stood up, too.

'In the meantime, I'm going to ask Rhett if he'll persuade you to stay.'

Sarah really didn't think that would help at all, but she didn't say what she thought. She just smiled and nodded before she made her way back to the house and began packing up her things.

Martin and his colleagues went out to dinner that evening. Sarah was grateful for that and she spent a quiet hour in the kitchen having her last meal with Beth.

'Is Lucy not eating with us tonight?' Sarah asked as she picked at the food on her plate, not feeling very hungry.

'She's eaten already and now she's helping Isobel to bath Harry,' Beth replied. 'He's such a handful.'

'It's going to be difficult for Isobel to manage without a professional nanny. What will she do?'

'I really don't know, I'm sure,' Beth said, shaking her head. 'My, what a strange week we've had. And now you're off tomorrow. I shall miss your company down here in the kitchen. We were getting used to you being around here.'

'I've enjoyed being here, too. You've all made me feel very welcome. I feel as though I've been here for far longer than ten days. I shall miss it.'

'I wonder what it will be like here

after that painting has been sold,' Beth contemplated, half to herself. 'I know Isobel has plans for the place. With all that money, things won't be the same again. I'm not sure it will be for the better, opening it to the public. Every Tom, Dick and Harry walking all over the place.'

Sarah smiled.

'You'll have me to blame for that, then. But if I hadn't discovered the painting the place would have just crumbled away. Not much of a legacy for Harry. I'm sure it won't be as bad as you think. Different, certainly, but you'll get used to it. Life does have a habit of changing. Sometimes there's nothing we can do about it.'

Beth sighed.

'You'll have to come back and see us sometime, when you're passing like.'

'I might just do that,' Sarah replied, but she didn't really think she ever would.

After dinner she helped Beth one last time with the dishes, then escaped again to the safe comfort of her room. Her suitcase lay packed on the bed and for all the meagre possessions it now contained, the room suddenly looked bare and uninviting. Several books were piled on the chair. Sarah knew she ought to return them to Fontingray's library, but she was afraid she might bump into Rhett. She would have liked a last look around the place, to wander through the rooms again by herself, take one last look and then lock all the memories away, but she remained in her room. It was the safest thing to do.

She had entertained the ridiculous notion that during the course of the evening Rhett would come steaming into her room and beg her to stay. Sarah had no idea if Isobel had talked to him or not, but if she had and he still did not want to come to try and change her mind, well, that spoke volumes and all she could do was accept the situation and try and walk away without crying over him.

Unlike the evening of her arrival, the

Fontingray peacocks were out in force next morning, strutting about as Sarah prepared to leave. Sam was helping to carry things out to the car for her and Beth was insisting that she ate a cooked breakfast.

It was mid-morning before she was ready to set off. She tried to tell herself that she wasn't deliberately taking her time in the vague hope that Rhett would appear at the eleventh hour. But that only happened in fairy tales and she knew fairies didn't exist.

There was no sign of Rhett or Martin but Isobel and Hugh came to see her off, with Harry. Beth and Lucy were there, too. They were lining the steps and as Sarah's car began to move away down the drive they waved then turned back into the house. She felt an enormous anti-climax. Isobel had apologised for Rhett not being there, too. She was obviously disappointed in her son for his lack of manners and had no idea how Sarah was really feeling about his absence.

'Please, don't apologise for him,' Sarah had said. 'I do understand. He's probably engrossed in his writing and it would be very unwise to interrupt his creative flow.'

She drove slowly. Her farewell party disappeared as she rounded the first corner in the drive. She almost couldn't bear to drive past the gatehouse, but it was the only way out. She looked up at the windows. Are you there, she wondered. Are you watching me leave?

She was almost at the main gate now, just one more bend in the drive. As she rounded it she almost stalled the car. Rhett was sitting on one of the boulders that lined the gravelled drive. He stood up as she came into view and stood in the middle of the road, flagging her down. She was so surprised she almost forgot how to stop the car and brought it to a halt only feet away from him. He walked around to the window and she wound it down.

'You're off then?' he said.

Sarah tried to keep her voice steady,

but her words came out shakily.

'Yes. I . . . er . . . I've finished everything I came to do.'

'Everything?' he asked.

It was a loaded question, full of innuendo and it made Sarah's stomach do another somersault.

'I'm not staying for the auction if that's what you mean,' she said.

'I understand my mother has offered you a job.'

'I haven't accepted it.'

'Why not?'

'The reason shouldn't concern you,' Sarah said, aware that she was shaking and her bottom lip was in danger of quivering.

'Would you reconsider?' he asked.

'No.'

'Get out of the car,' he snapped.

'I beg your pardon.'

He just stared at her. She got out, and felt her knees begin to buckle as he took her in his arms and kissed her.

'Now will you reconsider?' he said,

kissing the tip of her nose, her eyes, her neck.

'Yes, yes,' she said. 'OK, I will. I thought you'd never ask.'

'Better late than never,' he said.

'What made you change your mind about me?'

'Martin,' he replied.

'Martin?'

'When we were arranging for someone to come to Fontingray, Martin said he would send us his best and he was full of praise for you, said you were brilliant. He also said he was going to marry you. When you arrived I had a bit of a shock, you reminded me so much of Bridie. I fell for you but I remembered what Martin had said. I thought you were spoken for. When I realised you were flirting with me I couldn't make you out. I wasn't sure what you were up to.'

He paused and Sarah frowned.

'So what changed?'

'I saw what happened between the two of you in the Hall, you know, when he proposed. It changed everything.'

Sarah laughed.

'You were spying on me again from the minstrels' gallery.'

Rhett held up his hands.

'Guilty.'

'If I do stay and take the job,' she said, 'the first thing I'm going to do is dismantle the minstrels' gallery.'

'Hey, you can't do that,' he joked. 'It's a listed building. Besides, I thought you were all for restoration.'

'I am,' she said, 'and you've just restored my faith in men.'

'I have?'

'Most definitely,' she said, leaning against the car, looking back up the drive. 'I didn't get very far, did I?'

'I'm glad I timed it right and stopped you.'

'I'm glad, too, but it's going to be difficult staying on with Martin still here for the auction. I couldn't possibly face him.'

Rhett rubbed his chin and pretended to be deep in thought.

'Let's go back to the gatehouse and discuss the matter over a cup of coffee.'

Sarah smiled.

'What a good idea. Have you got any clean mugs though, or are they all stuck to the table again?'

Laughing happily, they walked hand in hand towards the gatehouse.

THE END